DRAGON'S PLIGHT

A ZEKE PHOENIX SUPERNATURAL THRILLER
BOOK 2

JOHN P. LOGSDON
ORLANDO A. SANCHEZ

CRIMSON MYTH
PRESS

Published by: Crimson Myth Press (www.CrimsonMyth.com)

Cover Art: Audrey Logsdon (www.AudreyLogsdon.com)

Thanks to TEAM ASS!
Advanced Story Squad

This is the first line of readers of the series. Their job is to help us keep things in check and also to make sure we're not doing anything way off base in the various story locations!

(listed in alphabetical order by first name)

Bennah Phelps
Dana Arms Audette
Debbie Tily
Hal Bass
Ian Nick Tarry
Jan Gray
Janice Kelly
Jodie Stackowiak
John Debnam
Kevin Frost
Larry Diaz Tushman
Megan McBrien
Mike Helas
Natalie Fallon
Penny Campbell-Myhill
Rob Hill
Sandee Lloyd
Scott Reid
Sharon Harradine
Tehrene Hart

Thanks to Team DAMN
Demented And Magnificently Naughty

This crew is the second line of readers who get the final draft of the story, report any issues they find, and do their best to inflate our fragile egos.

(listed in alphabetical order by first name)

Adam Goldstein, Alan Robert Bruce, Anne Morando, Audrey Cienki, Barbara Hamm, Barbara Henninger, Beth Adams, Bonnie Dale Keck, Carol Evans, Carolyn Fielding, Chris Christman II, Cindy D, Darren Musson, David Botell, Dorothy MPG, Emma Porter, Helen Day, Ingrid Shijven, Jacky Oxley, Jim Stoltz, Jen Cooper, Jen Stubbs, Julie Peckett, Kathleen Portig, Laura Cadger Rogers, LeAnne Benson, MaryAnn Sims, Melissa Parsons, Michelle Reopel, Myles, Penny Noble, Sara Mason Branson, Scott Ackerman, Stacey Stein, Stephen Bassett, Steve Widner, Terri Adkisson, Tom Intiso, Tony Dawson, Zak Klepek.

CHAPTER 1

$\mathcal{M}$y job was going to kill me.

I looked at the mountain of paper on my desk with a sigh. Two weeks had passed since my team and I explosively redecorated the Tower owned by Rake Masters and the Company, and most of the rank and file were in awe that we were still breathing.

We had a shortage of officers, and it was my job to reinforce the ranks with interviews and a never-ending pile of paper.

The stack of forms was typical for a Paranormal Police Department chief, or so I was informed by my second-in-command, Rose. Francisly, it seemed like Rose and the rest of my team just wanted to get away from this mind-numbing paperwork.

I was new to the position, which meant I was still learning. I needed people like Rose to guide me, even if she usually pointed me toward my doom. It made sense though. Being new to the position meant I had much to learn, it also meant non-stop hazing, usually in the form of some lethal prank—like a funeral party.

A knock at the door brought me out of my thoughts.

I glanced away from the main room in the station house just as Rose walked in.

She looked at the impressive stack of headaches on my desk and nodded, a small smirk framing her lips. She was dressed in her usual 'I came to kick ass' uniform. Black combat armor and dark glasses only added to the air of menace she carried around like a badge of honor.

To be fair, Rose was a hellion.

I checked my planner. "Is there a war on the schedule that I wasn't informed about?"

"Nothing wrong with being prepared," Rose answered. "And I'm always prepared."

She was a thin, ferocious-looking woman. Her resting 'kill' face kept most of the PPD away from her. That and the fact that hellions aren't known for their cheerful dispositions. Today, she had her shoulder-length blond hair pulled back in a tight ponytail. I noticed the small dagger that she had tucked into her ponytail keeping her hair in place. Even though it looked decorative, I knew that in her hands that little gem was lethal.

Despite the fact that she walked around perpetually pissed, Rose cared about the PPD and her team.

Fortunately, she'd grown to accept me as well. Why? I'd survived the funeral party usually thrown for new chiefs, which, in her eyes meant I went from target to grudgingly tolerated.

I remembered Hilda's words. She was the valkyrie who had adopted me at a young age. She'd said, *"Today's enemy is tomorrow's friend."* She then unsheathed her blade. *"If they are still enemies tomorrow—stab them with your sword and call it a day. This is the valkyrie way."*

"I'm not a valkyrie," I had replied.

"A pity, really. Remember, not every friend has your best interests at heart. Also, remember that not every enemy wants to destroy you."

"I wish that made sense."

"It will—one day. For now, dodge or die."

Being raised by valkyries was a never ending near-death experience. After the PPD's last run in with the Company and Masters' minions, Rose and I had come to an understanding of sorts. She'd stop trying to actively retire me, and I'd reconsider shooting her every chance I got.

It was working out so far.

She dropped into the chair opposite my desk and flung a bottle at me. I caught it. One of the benefits of being a dragon are the reflexes. I shoved one of the piles of paper to one side and pulled out two cups from a drawer.

"Percy says hello," Rose announced, leaning back in the chair. "Sent you that."

Percy owned and ran the Dirty Goblin, my one and only favorite drinking hole on the strip.

"Blood Ale," I cooed, opening the bottle. "Nice. Have time for a drink?"

"Only reason I brought the bottle over," Rose answered, putting her feet up on my desk and pointing at the paperwork. "Little bastard said he'd call to make sure you got it."

"Percy is many things," I answered, pouring the Blood Ale. "Little isn't one of them."

Rose grabbed the cup and emptied half the contents in a single gulp. Her eyes didn't even water.

Impressive.

"Looks like you're making progress," she said, and then downed the rest of the Blood Ale and looked at the glass. "Smooth as a hellion's bottom."

I wasn't about to ask precisely how smooth a hellion's bottom was.

"If, by progress, you mean I only want to drive a hot iron into one of my eyes, instead of two, then yes, I've made loads of progress."

"Perks of being the chief," she said with a smirk. "Any threats on your life lately?"

"Besides the one where I have a hellion for a partner?"

"That's called an occupational hazard," Rose answered. "You'll get used to it...eventually."

"These weeks feel like years," I said, pinching the bridge of my nose. "I think it's the paperwork that kills PPD chiefs."

"At least you survived the funeral party."

"Yay," I sighed.

Rose raised her glass in salute. "You are in the rarefied company of chiefs who have made it more than one week."

"How many is that?"

"Not sure," Rose said, pensively. "Two, I think? They didn't last the month, which means...goals. Anyway, congrats."

"Thank you, I think."

"Sure," she said, pouring herself another glass of Blood Ale. "The main hurdle is over. Now, it'll be just regular attempts on your life."

"Can't wait."

She put the bottle of Blood Ale back on the desk. I snagged it and began gulping, bypassing the glass completely.

CHAPTER 2

*A*nother knock on the door.

"Package for you, Chief," said one of the officers carrying a medium-sized box. "No return address."

"Shit," Rose said, jumping to her feet. "Move back and call Nimble."

"Are we not supposed to get boxes here?" I asked, confused at her response. "It's just—"

"Were you not paying attention?" Rose huffed. "Bombs and explosive devices fall under the 'regular death threats' category."

Rose had stepped away and was backing out of the office.

I tried to connect to Nimble, the lead technician at the Badlands PPD, but I couldn't get through.

"Rowena," I said through my connector, *"connect me to Nimble."*

Rowena and I were on better terms. I didn't have to preface her name with her royal title anymore, but I still had to address her by her proper name. I had yet to get the hang of using the AI as well as the rest of the team.

"One moment, Chief."

I backed away from the box and headed into the corridor.

"He was busily applying ooze to his exterior," Rowena said, finally. *"Connecting you now."*

Nimble was a slug. That meant he had to constantly keep himself covered in goop, or he'd end up drying out.

"Hello, Chief Phoenix," he said.

"Nimble," I said, *"we have a strange box in my office."*

"Congratulations, things must really be slow if this is the highlight of your day, Chief."

"Rose seems to think this could be an explosive."

"Hmmm," he replied, his voice turning serious. *"This strange box you speak of...is it making noise?"*

"None that I can hear," I said. *"Let's get EOD to my office —now."*

Rose had moved to the other end of the corridor.

"Explosive Ordinance Disposal is on their way," Nimble said. *"Can you describe the box? What makes it strange?"*

Rose and I looked at each other and shrugged.

"Nothing to say really," I answered. *"It's very...boxlike?"*

"Definitely boxlike," agreed Rose. *"No doubt about it being a box."*

"No return address," I added.

"That's a bad sign," Nimble answered. *"It could well be an explosive."*

"Exactly why we contacted you," I noted. *"What's the protocol for potential explosives against a PPD chief?"*

"We usually take a pool to see which body part gets blown

off first. I think Graffon is the leader in that pool. Would you like me to confirm?"

"No, I meant PPD protocol."

"Oh, it's not too complicated," Nimble answered. *"If we determine it's an explosive—and it usually is where chiefs are concerned—we make sure to employ ground based high-velocity in the opposite direction of said device to clear the immediate area."*

"So...you run away?"

"Precisely," he confirmed. *"The team should be arriving any second."*

A group of three PPD officers dressed in bomb suits came down the corridor. They held blast shields, sealed off the area, and installed a bomb barricade.

"These guys are brave," I said to Rose. She stood around the corner from my office now.

"Brave?" Rose asked. "Playing with a bomb is not brave. That's called suicidal insanity."

"Do you really think it's a bomb?" I asked. "It could just be a regular package."

Rose removed her glasses and glared at me. "You're the chief," she said. "Who do you know who would want to send you a package? Do you have friends? Unlikely. Close acquaintances? Doubtful. That only leaves one thing: enemies."

"I could have friends," I said, fighting to keep the hurt from my voice. "You don't know."

"If there was a remote chance that you did have friends, that friendship dissolved on the day you became chief," Rose answered. "No one wants to be friends with a PPD chief. It shortens life expectancy."

"So, it's a bomb."

"I think it's something designed to end your life, which means no proximity right now." She crossed over and stood on the other side of the corridor. "Let's just respect each other's personal space for now, in case whatever that thing is has homing capabilities."

One of the EOD officers entered my office slowly.

"E1 approaching container now," the officer said as he approached the box. "E2, I'm going to need the Tactical Operational Neutralizing Grappling Sleeve."

"You sure, sir?" E2 answered. "Is it that bad?"

E1 nodded. "Better to be safe. Would hate for this thing to detonate the chief—when he's so far away."

"You had arms, too?" E2 asked. "Yeah, most we can get now is shrapnel damage. That you E3?"

"This chief is smart," E3 said with a nod. "He'd at least get a few feet away before it exploded on him. Shrapnel FTW."

"My earlier assessment of them being brave was off," I said, looking at Rose. "I meant they were brave assholes."

"Let's go E2," E1 said with a hand outstretched. "Don't have all day."

The second EOD officer reached into a bag and pulled out a large pair of wooden cooking tongs.

"What the hell is that?" I asked. "Those are just tongs. I have a pair just like that in my kitchen."

All three EOD officers stopped and looked in my direction.

"Not like these," E2 answered, handing the tongs to E1. "These are Tactical Operational—"

"Cut the shit," I said. "Those are *tongs*."

E1 shook his head and took the tongs. "Amateurs," he said. "Everyone's an expert until things blow up in their face. Then it's 'Help, I can't find my arm!' or 'Where's my leg?'"

"Ain't that the truth," E2 said, looking in my direction and shaking his head. "Why don't you let the professionals handle this, sir?"

I glanced at Rose who was deliberately ignoring me. "That's just a pair of tongs," I said. "Are they kidding me?"

"These guys are professionals. Let them work, unless you want to go over there and have a blast with whatever is in that box?"

"Pass," I said. "Doesn't mean they aren't using a plain old pair of tongs, though."

"Does it matter?" Rose asked. "You call your shotguns Pinky and Butterfly."

Muffled giggles came from the EOD officers, and I swore I overheard one of them say 'Pinky and Butterfly', followed by more laughter.

I shook my head. I wasn't going to explain my weapon's names to these idiots.

E1 snapped up the box with the tongs and held out his hand again.

"I'm going to need a Kinetic Null Incision Force Expander—now."

"Shit, E1," E2 said, reaching into the bag and pulling out a small knife. "Are you sure?"

"That...is...a...knife!" I yelled. "What the fu—?"

"Sir!" E2 said, holding up a hand. "If you can't keep calm, we're going to have you removed from the area. You don't see us telling you how to be chief, do you? Let us do our job."

I looked at Rose who shrugged back at me.

"Ridiculous," I said, moving back as E3 pointed down the corridor. "Fine, I'm moving."

E1 proceeded to use the knife to open the box and look inside. That's when I heard the beeping.

"Good news and bad news, sir," E1 said from my office. "Which would you like first?"

"You have got to be joking me," I said, barely controlling my anger. "Good news or bad news?"

"Well?" E1 asked, glancing down at the box. "I wouldn't take all day."

"Give me the good news," I said, my voice on edge. "What is it?"

"Well...I can tell what it's not." He lifted a large hockey-puck shaped item from the box. "*This* is not an explosive."

"What's the bad news?" I asked.

"It appears to be an Empiric trigger, and you have roughly thirty minutes to find out what it detonates." He turned the trigger, and I saw a timer counting down from twenty-nine minutes.

"Well," E2 said, packing up, "our job here is done. We're out."

"Your job is done?" I asked in disbelief. "What about the trigger?"

"Sir," E1 said, "we are an Explosive Ordinance Disposal team. There no explosives present, which means there is nothing to dispose of. You have a good day."

"Excuse me?" I said, raising my voice. "You aren't going to look for what that thing detonates?"

E1 turned to me. "What you need is the EDU—the Explosive Discovery Unit. That's what they do."

"EDU?" It took everything I had not to go partial dragon on these idiots. "Fine. Where are they?"

"Gone, sir," E1 said, resting a hand over his heart. E2 and E3 mimicked his gesture. "They discovered a large explosive—"

"Let me guess," I said. "They had no way of disposing of it before it exploded."

"Blown to hell," E2 said, catching himself and looking at Rose. "Not literally of course, no offense ma'am."

"You 'ma'am' me again and I'll send your parts to hell," Rose growled. "Get out of here. You're useless."

The EOD team moved as fast as their suits would allow.

"Sir," Nimble's voice came over my connector, "we may have a situation."

CHAPTER 3

I moved fast into my office and grabbed the trigger.

"*I'm holding an Empiric trigger,*" I said. "*But we don't know what it triggers. I don't have any Empirics here.*"

"*Well, that answers my question,*" Nimble said. "*We just received a new shipment of Empiric explosives. They're in the armory.*"

I swallowed hard.

"*Are you saying these things are connected?*"

"*Well,*" Nimble said after a long pause, "*is your trigger counting down from twenty-three minutes and forty seconds? Thirty-nine...thirty-eight...*"

I looked at the timer on the trigger and a knot of fear punched me in the stomach.

"*Yes, why?*"

"*Every Empiric in the armory is active and counting down.*"

That wasn't good. I knew damn well what a single Empiric was capable of, but latching them together into one mega-Empiric? Yikes.

"How many are there, and can we contain them?"

"They are contained—in the armory," Nimble said. *"I'm locking down the weapons cache now. I'd suggest getting out of the building while you still can. Once I have this locked down, we're leaving."*

"How many Empirics do we have in the armory currently?"

"Enough to level two of these stations and have some left over for an attractive crater," Nimble answered. *"If this blast door doesn't hold, the Badlands PPD will be homeless in a few minutes."*

"Holy hell," I said aloud. "We need to get everyone out of here."

"We need to evacuate the station," Rose called out, pulling a lever on a small box near the office. "Everybody out! Now!"

Red emergency lights shone in all of the corridors as klaxons blared. Most of the officers were doing a great impression of running in circles as they tried to exit the station. It was clear they had no clue about how to evacuate in an emergency situation.

"Don't we drill for these kind of scenarios?" I asked, looking around at the lack of coordination. "These officers are clueless."

"Drill?" Rose asked. "What kind of budget do you think we have? You're lucky if they find their way to their desks everyday."

She was right. I'd seen the reports. The problem was the crew had to get out before this thing detonated, or, more accurately, *caused* the detonations.

"Can't we disable the trigger?" I asked, holding up the hockey-puck in my hand. "Can we turn this thing off?"

Rose looked at me. "Do *you* know how to do that?" She grabbed the weapons from her desk. "I sure as hell don't, and I'm not going to learn in"—she turned the trigger I held to look at the screen—"in twenty minutes. But hey, knock yourself out. I think there's a copy of *Demolitions and Disarms* lying around here somewhere."

"Where are you going?" I asked in the midst of the chaos. "You said it yourself, the people have no clue how to evacuate."

"Me? I'm getting as far away as I can get in twenty minutes."

I sighed at her and grimaced.

"Nimble, do we have an evacuation plan in place?"

"Of course," he answered. *"Everyone finds a door and exits the building."*

Right.

There was no way I could evacuate the entire building on my own, but I could get my team to help as best they can.

"Rose," I commanded, *"coordinate officers to the exits near us, that's an order."*

"Fuck!" Rose shot back over the comms and started barking orders at the crew.

A few seconds later, shots rang out, freezing the men in place.

"Next person who ignores me gets shot," she yelled. "Now, this way! Move it! Double time!"

The cops followed her directions immediately.

I opened up a group channel to my direct crew.

"Alpha Team, we need to get as many people out as possible"—I looked down at the trigger—*"you have nineteen*

minutes to clear the building and get yourselves to safety. Every Empiric in the armory is going to go off in that time."

"Affirmative, Chief," their voices came back. *"Rendezvous at rally point A."*

I grabbed my coat and my shotguns, Pinky & Butterfly, and ran into the corridor. The offices on my floor were empty.

No one pissed off a hellion, at least not deliberately.

Rose had cleared them all. I ran down the hallway, letting my senses expand to make sure there weren't any stragglers. It was clear. I headed for the stairwell, pressing Whoosh, the ring I wore to help control how far into dragon form I changed. My wings formed, allowing me an extra burst of speed as I climbed the stairs.

Minutes were shaving off the countdown as I scanned floor after floor, looking for anyone who had yet to get the memo. There were so many side rooms and storage closets, that I just didn't have the time to check everywhere. While the Badlands Paranormal Police Department was not exactly known for having a massive number of officers, the building could have housed a few hundred. That meant everyone was spread out among the multiple floors, taking advantage of windowed offices wherever possible.

I managed to scour up to the third floor before the trigger chimed and showed a three minute countdown.

Something told me that there were stragglers in the damn building.

There wasn't much I could do at this point. If people weren't listening through the connector, or simply didn't believe there was a genuine threat, then Darwinism would rule the day.

With a growl, I took off toward the roof as fast as my body would allow, kicking open the access door. I ran for the edge, leaping over it.

Rally point A was a meeting area about half a mile away. It was designated a safe distance in case of an explosive attack. I covered the distance in under a minute, landing near my team.

I saw only about half of the building personnel had been evacuated.

Shit.

Maybe they were on the other side?

Wishful thinking, likely, but it was all I had to hang my hat on.

Then the remote showed thirty seconds remained. I held the device up so everyone in the vicinity could see it.

As one, they all turned to look at the Badlands PPD HQ.

"Rowena," I said, "*contact Fire Control. Tell them we may have an emergency at the station. Get some Medevacs ready as well.*"

"*Affirmative,*" she responded. "*Contacting all first responders.*"

"What's the range on these things?" I said, lowering the device as it counted down to zero. "Maybe we're too far for it to send the signal?"

"Effective range, is two miles with uninterrupted line of sight," Tam said from behind me. "We're well within range."

"Don't forget the signal repeater towers," Yarrl added.

"Effective range taking into account signal boost, is closer to three miles."

"Does that make a difference?" I asked.

"Irrelevant," Tam said. "Once activated, no one has ever successfully managed to deactivate an empiric explosive."

Tam and Yarrl were two hellion lab techs who were tasked with assisting and protecting Nimble while he worked on his projects. Yarrl, the male, was about my height and muscular. I'm sure he could hold his own against most things in the Badlands without breaking a sweat. Tam, the female, was shorter and slim. Her eyes held an old, quiet, menace. She gave off a subtle vibe of 'invade my personal space and die,' which explained why no one got too close to her.

"You're right," Tam said, squinting out over the distance at the Badlands PPD HQ. "The only question now is: will the blast door hold?"

The timer counted down to zero with another chime. I winced, expecting the station to go up in a ball of flame, but nothing happened.

"Maybe it malfunctioned?" I asked, optimistically. "Is it possible this one was a dud?"

"Statistically unlikely," Nimble noted. He was wearing a plastic covering that kept his sensitive skin covered in goop. There was a small hole where his face and eye-stalks popped through. He was riding on a wheeled device of some sort, too. It had clearly been made specifically for his unique physique. "The distance means there will be some lag."

The next second all of the windows in the building

shattered, followed by a series of tremors that knocked us clear off our feet. Nimble's vehicle compensated, allowing him to stay upright.

"You'd better get those first responders over there, Chief," Nimble said quietly.

CHAPTER 4

The Badlands PPD Station looked like someone had used it for artillery practice. Some of the walls had huge holes in them, and I saw chunks of debris everywhere.

We stood in the makeshift command center on the outer perimeter of the destruction. The center was a group of temporary structures, tents really, put up by Fire Control and the Medevacs. Our area, designated for PPD Command, held my Alpha Team and other PPD officers performing logistics and coordinating duties.

Doe, our resident void, and Graffon, a demonoid, prepared to give me an assessment.

It was all I could do not to run away.

Voids, or faceless ones, were found on the fifth level of hell. That was the level of wrath. They were known for getting into your head, making you suffer through mental torment, depression, and downright lunacy. It was the rare individual who could make it past that level.

Demons were essentially attorneys, though even

scarier. They were tough, ruthless, powerful, and exacting. A demon would eat you just as soon as look at you, unless you were protected by a contract, or if they owed you one.

"How bad is it?" I asked the pair, looking outside at the damage and taking a shot of Blood Ale. I was surprised the building was still standing. "It looks bad."

"Seems to me that the building is about to collapse," Doe said in his monotone voice, making his veil, and the unicorn printed on it, bounce. "Maybe we should place some charges and finish the job. We've been wanting new offices for some time now."

"And the people inside?" I asked. "What about them?"

"I believe that's why we have hazard pay in our contracts," Doe answered. "They knew the risks when they signed up."

"Absolutely not," I answered, averting my gaze from Doe—just in case.

A full-on void would have to wear a veil to protect others from falling into a pit of despair and self-loathing. They *could* also shut off their influence, allowing you to see their faces without risk, but it wasn't their default look. That made veils an important garb choice.

Graffon, who was a mix of void and demon, seemed unaffected by Doe. Even though she was half faceless, she managed to control that aura of endless despair and mental torment that the faceless walked around with. According to the personnel files, she was the only one who lasted more than a day as Doe's partner. Everyone else the PPD tried to pair him up with met a gruesome end.

"Well, sir," Graffon chimed in, "I'm not in construction, nor am I an engineer, although I do have a relative who practices construction contract law and I have extensively studied the Badlands Construction Regulations. However, it would appear, judging from the damage to the façade of the structure, that the entire edifice is approaching catastrophic failure. This, of course, is pure conjecture. It is, however, based on a solid observation of factors. According to Badlands Construction Regulation 14.793, subsection 7.2, tertiary division C dash 5, 'A building may be deemed hazardous and condemnable by the visual inspection of a licensed contractor or holder of a ratified Badlands Building Inspector badge. In the event that the building in question poses no immediate danger, corroborating opinions of three ratified inspectors are required to condemn the structure.'"

My eyes started to glaze over, my brain tuned her out as a purely defensive reflex. I checked my ears to make sure I wasn't bleeding, thankfully it was only sweat. I raised a hand to signal her to stop, but she continued, oblivious to the expression of pain on my face.

"Seeing that this is clearly a situation where the building has undergone an explosion," she continued, ignoring my attempt to stop her, "and noting that I am a ratified Badlands Building Inspector, I am authorized to make a judgement based on the aforementioned observable factors."

"That's swell, Graffon, but—"

"For example," she continued without pausing for a breath, "the distance the tremors had to travel to reach our location at the rally point was considerable, possessing enough force to knock us down, which can only mean the Empirics detonated and set off a chain explosion, destroying all of the weaponry within the armory. Furthermore, the fact that the entirety of the windows in the building are shattered, speaks to energy waves traveling at velocity to the apex of the structure."

That was interesting. Very interesting.

My brain revved back up from reverse to second gear.

"Repeat that part again," I said.

"All of this points to—"

"No, not that," I said, rubbing my temples while fighting off a Graffon-induced migraine. "What did you say before that?"

"I've said quite a few things," Graffon answered. "Can you elaborate on what specifically you would like me to reiterate? I do tend to provide a voluminous amount of content."

"Understatement of the century," Silk, our resident Dark fae, muttered. "She's never learned to get to the point."

"Leave her alone," Butch said. "Chief, do you want us to assist the Medevacs?"

The malkyrie towered over most of us, his armor glistening in the low light. I had a hard time understanding how the valkyries accepted a male into their ranks—then again, they did raise a dragon.

Anything was possible in the Badlands.

"Everyone except Graffon, Rose, and Nimble, assist the rescue effort immediately," I said. "We need to know how many were injured—get me those numbers, people."

"Yes, sir," they answered, filing out of the command

center. I turned to Graffon as the rest of the team headed off to find the Medevacs personnel.

"Once we're done here," I said, looking at her, "find the lead medical officer and assist in getting our people to safety."

"Will do, Chief," Graffon confirmed. "Considering the state of the building, some of the personnel will be exposed to infectious bacteria. We may have an epidemic on our hands. If that occurs, do I have authorization to quarantine the area and take measures to eliminate any threatening infection or virus?"

That was one of those loaded questions that I was getting used to hearing around here. I hadn't been the chief long enough to know the full lay of the land, but I was picking up on a few things.

"Exactly how would you do that?" I asked with a tilt of my head. "Get rid of the virus, I mean."

"By elimination of the host of course," Graffon answered, cheerfully. "We seal off the building with the infected personnel and then detonate the structure. It would be much like what our attackers had attempted, but handled surgically."

"As efficient as that sounds, please consult with me before taking any actions in that direction," I said. "Are we clear?"

"Absolutely," Graffon answered. "Just trying to cover every eventuality."

"Let's focus on the weapons—explain."

"I think I can shed some light there," Nimble chimed in. "If my calculations are right, and I won't be able to determine this until I return to what's left of the lab, it would seem all of the weapons are gone."

"Gone?" I asked. "What do you mean…gone?"

"As in non-existent," Nimble answered. "All of our weapons"—he lowered his voice—"are gone. Destroyed in the blast."

"So much for eradicating the infectious officers," Graffon mused.

I gave her a concerned glance before turning back to Nimble. "Can't we just go to the backup armory and replace the weapons?" His stalks wiggled, making me uncomfortable. "Tell me we have a backup armory with a fresh batch of weapons, Nimble."

"Okay," Nimble replied, "we have a backup armory with a fresh batch of weapons."

It was said in a way that made me think he was merely repeating what I'd asked him to repeat.

"*Do* we have a backup armory with a fresh batch of weapons?" I asked him, pointedly.

"We do not," he answered.

Rose raised an eyebrow and slowly shook her head.

"Graf," she said with a grunt, "why don't you go help out with the injured while we sort this out."

"Sure," Graffon replied. "Statistically the amount of injured is a direct correlation—"

"No one wants to hear it, Graf," Rose interrupted. "And note that I said *help* the injured, not make *more* injured. Keep the talking to a minimum."

"Got it," Graf said, running off to join the others.

I watched Graffon sprint off while trying to wrap my head around things. Here we were, in the middle of the most dangerous part of the world, including the combined naughty spots in the overworld, the Netherworld, and most sections of the Badlands...and we had no weapons?

It was all I could do to keep my frustration from showing.

"We don't have an offsite armory?" I asked.

"Well," Nimble began, "there are many ways you could look at things of this nature. First, I would suggest that we—"

"Yes or no, Nimble?"

"No."

"That's what I was afraid of," I groaned, knowing that I'd have to let him drone on about what we *did* have to work with. "Okay, break it down."

"There is nothing to break down, sir," Tam said from behind me.

Sneaking up on a dragon is next to impossible, and yet, both she and Yarrl did it with ease. I shook my head —hellions.

They remained in the Command Center, because, unlike my team, not only were they lab technicians, they were also required to protect Nimble at all times.

"Can we get to our weapons or not?" I asked.

"The armory blast door held for the most part, until the explosion became too much, then it failed. We only have one armory."

"So you're saying that we have no weapons?" I asked. That's when frustration won the day, causing me to repeat my feelings with a bit more volume. "We're in the Badlands PPD and we have no weapons?"

"Would you like a megaphone so you can make sure everyone around us can hear you?" Rose asked, glaring. "Keep it down, dipshit."

Dipshit?

I sneered, but said nothing in retaliation.

"That's not entirely true," Nimble piped up, after a few seconds. "We do have *some* weapons."

"Where?" I asked. "Rose and I can go get them."

"What weapons are you carrying?" Nimble asked. His stalks began moving up and down. "On your person, I mean."

"My shotguns," I answered, not sure where he was going with this. "I've also got six hundred rounds of ammo."

"You have six hundred rounds?" Rose asked, incredulously looking me over. "How the shit can you carry that many rounds? Do dragons have pouches?"

"I didn't say I was carrying them all on me," I answered. "I said I had six hundred rounds. Some I keep in the car, and Percy lets me keep some at the Dirty Goblin." I grimaced at her. "And, no, dragons do *not* have pouches."

Rose lifted my jacket. "What the hell do you need that many rounds for? Are we going to war?"

"In this instance," Nimble started, "the chief's exuberant stockpiling of ammunition is beneficial."

"Why is that?" I ventured with some hesitation.

"Because we only have the weapons we possess with us right now."

I *knew* that was coming. I just fucking knew it.

Who the hell thought that it would be a good idea to

bypass having a backup stash of weapons? It made no damn sense. I mean, sure, if we had been policing the antarctic topside, *maybe* it wouldn't have been such a big deal.

But we weren't!

We were in the flipping Badlands here!

"We're going to need more weapons," I stated, simmering, "and we are going to need to find them before this gets out to the rest of the Badlands."

"That may be...complicated," Nimble said. "The closest cache of weapons is in Netherworld Proper."

"That's not complicated," Rose laughed in a not-so-funny way. "That's fucking impossible."

CHAPTER 5

"We'd never make it," Rose announced. "Just think about what you're saying. A Netherworld Proper run, with a convoy packed full of weaponry, driven by the officers of the Paranormal Police Department…" She stopped and looked at us expectantly. "It's suicide."

"But that's where the weapons are," Nimble answered. "If we are in need of weaponry, we have little choice but to take the risk." Nimble's stalks looked directly at each other for a moment. He jumped and made a strange yelping sound, making it clear that he'd scared himself. "The deeper question that I have is," he added, recovering, "who attacked us in the first place?"

"He's the Chief," Rose said, pointing at me. "What makes you think this was directed at anyone else?"

"Granted, in most cases that would be enough of a reason," Nimble answered. "But the funeral party is over,"—Nimble pointed his stalks at me—"congratulations by the way."

"Thanks," I sighed, not certain that congratulations were really in order, all things considered.

"In my opinion," Nimble continued, "this was not directed solely at the chief. It was a specific attack against the PPD. It was focused on our capability to defend the Badlands."

"You said we received a shipment of Empirics recently?" I asked. "How recently?"

"Let me see," Nimble replied as ooze coated his datapad. I almost felt sorry for that poor piece of technology. "Last week."

"Were there other weapons in the same shipment?"

"No," he replied, looking confused. "That's rather odd, actually. In fact, we weren't due any weapon shipments for another month."

I nodded. "Is it possible to track who provided them?"

"I'll look into it," Rose said, taking out her datapad. "I should be able to get the delivery manifest."

Graffon reappeared at the entrance of the tent.

"What do you have for us?" I asked. "Updates?"

"Yes, sir," Graffon answered with a smile. "Half of the personnel sustained injuries, ranging from mild to severe. The critical cases are being rushed off-site by Medevacs."

"I don't think you should be smiling while you give that report, Graffon," I noted. "It may send the wrong impression."

"My apologies, Chief," Graffon answered, reducing the smile by half, making her look only mildly psychotic. "I was just contemplating the potential for legal claims against the PPD. This is a demon's best worst-case scenario."

"Right," I said, making a mental note to get Graffon out more often. "What about the lab where the weapons were stored?"

"That would be Silk's area," she answered.

"*Silk,*" I called through the connector, "*how is the lab where the weapons were stored?*"

"*Completely slagged,*" she replied. "*The explosion melted everything. The good news is that the building isn't going to collapse into a pile of rubble. Engineers say structural integrity is solid, but we're looking at months, if not years, of repairs.*"

"*Thanks, Silk.*" I shut off the connection. "Silk says that the lab is toast, but that the building can be fixed. It's just going to take a fair bit of time."

"Again, Chief," Graffon stated, "I could condemn it. It's within my rights as a—"

"No, no," I interrupted with a sigh. "We're not condemning the building. It's in pretty bad shape, but at least it won't collapse." I took a deep breath. "I'm going to need to speak to the Directors."

"Indeed," Nimble agreed. "They do need to be briefed as well. As I'm sure you've surmised, this situation will escalate quickly if we are unarmed."

"Imagine that, the PPD unarmed in the Badlands," I scoffed. "Why don't we just walk around with signs that say 'shoot me now'? It'd be easier."

I stepped out of the tent.

"*Rowena, can you connect me with the Directors?*"

"*Failed the link is,*" Rowena gargled on the group channel. "*Comply with request I cannot.*"

"Nimble," Rose asked, irritated, "what is wrong with your girlfriend? She sounds scrambled."

Nimble slithered over to the shade of a tent and began tapping quickly on his datapad.

"This is bad," he said. "The explosion must have caused this."

"What happened to it?" I asked. His eyestalks glared at me. "Her. Not 'it.' I meant what happened to *her*?"

"It seems to be a Dyao Syntactic corruption," Nimble answered, still tapping away. "It must have been the blast. That's the only logical explanation."

"How would an explosion affect an AI?" I asked. "I mean it…sorry, *she* doesn't exist 'anywhere'?"

"Her main server was adjacent to the lab," Nimble answered. "It probably exploded along with the weapons."

"Was there anything else down there we need to be worried about?"

"Plenty," Nimble said. "All of it above your pay-grade. Rowena is the only thing that impacts the PPD directly."

"I see," I said. "Where is she now? How can she still communicate if her server is gone?"

"I have a backup server off-site for eventualities like this."

"Why does she sound backwards?"

"Her method of communication has become anastrophic. It's highly unusual."

"Damn right, it's catastrophic," I said, frustrated that our main method of communication was malfunctioning. "Why does she sound like she's choking on blood ale?"

"She sounds like she's choking on something a lot harder than blood ale," Silk said with a chuckle. "Hey, slug, do you and your girlfriend—you know, bump digital eyestalks or whatever it is slugs do?"

"Anastrophic is not the same as catastrophic," Nimble corrected me, ignoring Silk. "I had a test server that I was doing some basic development on. Just a fun operating system whereby the normal word order of the subject, verb, and object gets changed. I called it the Yobibyte Origination Dialect Anastrophimizer."

"Y.O.D.A.?" asked Rose, rolling her eyes.

"Precisely," Nimble beamed. "I just hadn't expected Rowena to escape there. I'll need to relocate her to a larger, more stable server."

"They always prefer it larger, slug," Silk said. "Trust me, size matters."

It was my turn to ignore Silk.

"How long will that take?" I asked. "And can we shut her off in the meantime?"

"This is a finesse job," Nimble answered after a pause. "I don't want to do anything rash here. This has to be done carefully, gently."

"Make sure you use plenty of lube," Silk said. "That way you won't have to use the force. You can *ease* it in."

I swore I heard Butch giggle.

"Shut it for a second, Silk," I said with a sigh. The headache was threatening to pound my brain out of my ears. "How long, Nimble?"

"A few days, a week at most," he said.

"So she can jump from one computer to another in an instant," Rose questioned, "but it'll take you a week to move her to yet another one?"

"It's more complicated moving her from the Y.O.D.A. because of the way the system was developed," he defended. "Again, I never expected her to land there.

Anyway, just let me worry about Rowena and the tech. In the meantime, you need to figure out how to replenish our manpower and weapons."

I looked at him. "Manpower?"

"He's right," Rose said. "We're at half-strength, based on the injury reports. Right now, any number of insignificant criminal groups on the Strip outnumber us, forget about the Company. If they attacked now, they could wipe out the PPD."

"The Company," I said. "You think Masters could be behind this?"

"You mean like a huge 'fuck you very much for blowing up my Tower' kind of gesture?" Rose asked, pensively. "Seems a little elaborate, even for him."

"But not out of the question," I countered. "He seemed like the type that wouldn't let the explosion go unanswered."

"True, it's worth checking out," Rose said. "Silk and Butch, go around to the Tower and see what you can dig up. Whereabouts and activity."

"Last I saw they were still mid-construction after the explosion," I said. "Try The Company HQ as well."

"Masters won't let them get past the property line at Gorgon's," Rose said. "Try the Tower first, then see if you can find out anything at the complex. If it gets too hot, back off and regroup on us."

Silk and Butch left the tent.

"Who's the next in line of command after our team?" I asked.

"That would be Crenshaw, but he was crushed in the

explosion," Rose said. "Next would be Lieutenant Robbens."

"Anton was slammed in the head by a slab of concrete," Graffon pointed out. "Doctors say it's serious. He's been wanting to help everyone work through their issues by talking to them ever since."

"Ugh, acute guruenteritis," Rose spat, shaking her head. "No cure and not usually fatal, unless the person they're trying to 'help' attacks them. Hope they caught it in time."

"Who does that leave?" I asked. "Who would be next?"

"That would be Lieutenant Bradley, Chief," Graffon said. "He is acting captain when Alpha Team is in the field."

"Is he among the injured?"

"No, sir," Graffon answered sadly. "He evacuated with only minor scratches and bruises."

"Good, get him to my office," I commanded, heading back in to the station. "We need to discuss the recruitment of our new PPD officers."

"And the weapons?" Graffon asked. "That's kind of important, sir."

"Again, I need to speak to the Directors."

CHAPTER 6

J made it inside the station without having to clear security.

At this point, if anyone wanted to take down the Badlands PPD, all they needed was a small, determined group of moderately armed individuals. That described almost every criminal organization on the Strip at the moment. Except The Company. They were a large, determined group of *heavily* armed individuals.

We needed to get more weapons and personnel.

The interior of the station was doing an excellent imitation of a warzone. Dust was everywhere. Shards of glass were scattered all over the floors. Many of the doors hung open, their frames knocked askew by the explosion.

My confidence in the integrity of the building was shaken when I saw the gaping craters in the walls revealing the internal framework. I made room for the First Responders and medical personnel running around the floor. Nimble, Rose, and the others remained downstairs in the PPD Command Center.

Director calls were live calls, in a hidden office, and for chiefs only. In the midst of all the destruction, the door to my office managed to suffer little damage. I opened it and noticed the stark difference.

My office had made it through the explosion unscathed. Apparently the structural integrity of the Chief's office was reinforced to protect the Director's Hub. My office wasn't overly large. A tall filing cabinet sat to one side of the room. A good-sized desk sat in the center of the room. The desk held a computer and the stacks of officer forms I wasn't looking forward to reviewing. There was also a phone.

"Rowena," I said with a pause, "is the Director Hub still functional?"

A feedback whine pierced through my brain before settling down.

"Operational the Hub is, survived the explosion it did."

Nimble was going to have to fix her—and soon.

I still thought it was inefficient to have the Chief be physically present for these calls, but I understood the security concerns.

"On the wall the panel is," Rowena said. "Access it grants. Biometrics the key."

"Got it, thanks," I said quickly to stop the mixed up speech. "I remember."

I placed my hand on the wall, and a panel slid to the side revealing a small room with a desk, a large comfortable chair, and three monitors attached to the far wall. There was nothing else in there. Above each monitor was a name placard.

Taragon in the center, Ellium to the left, and Long to the right.

I sat in the chair, and the monitors turned on. Silhouetted and obscured figures appeared in each of the monitors. There was no way I'd remember their faces, especially since I couldn't really see them. I knew that they were representatives from each of the major three factions, dragon, hellion, and denizens of hell. Long was the dragon, Ellium was with the hellions, and Taragon represented hell. What I couldn't tell was what gender they were or any other identifying characteristic.

This made sense, seeing that a Director of the PPD in the Badlands would make for a wonderful target. Just remember the welcome I got as the Chief, and you can likely imagine what a Director's entourage would entail.

"Update, Chief Ezekias," said Long. "We understand the station has just suffered an explosion. Are there any causalities?"

"Don't you mean casualties?"

"Those as well," interjected Ellium. "Was this an attack?"

"It's beginning to look that way," I affirmed, "but we have a bigger problem."

"What could be worse than the building exploding?" Long asked. "How many are hurt?"

"Half of the PPD personnel are hurt or incapacitated in some way."

"Half?" Taragon asked. "How did you let this happen?"

"*Let* this happen?" I asked taking a long breath and counting to ten. "How was I supposed to prevent it?"

"You're the chief," Ellium said, "and a dragon. I would

think you have a distinct advantage when it comes to fire and explosives."

I refrained from ripping the monitor off the wall and shredding it; instead, I opted to take another breath and gather myself.

"We have a bigger issue at hand," I said again, looking at all of the monitors. "Something more pressing than the attack on the building."

"I fail to see what could be more pressing," Taragon started. "As chief, the Badlands PPD is your responsibility. You have a duty to perform, its imperative—"

"All of the weapons are gone."

Silence from the monitors.

Even their pixellated faces were mostly still.

"I've experienced inept leadership in the past, but this...this is staggering," Ellium said, finally. "You managed to *lose* all of the weapons?"

"I didn't *lose* them," I replied, restraining myself from unloading both shotguns into the monitors. "The trigger set off all the Empirics in our armory. The blast destroyed all of the weapons."

"Who sent the trigger?" Taragon asked. "Do you know?"

"Rose is tracking it down as we speak."

"The hellion?" Long asked. "Is that prudent?"

"What's that supposed to mean, Long?" asked Ellium with some heat.

"Just that dragons are better suited for this type of sleuthing, Ellium."

Ellium scoffed. "Your boy here is a dragon and he's lost

all the weapons and put the entire Badlands PPD in jeopardy!"

I assumed *I* was the 'boy' in that statement. This became more apparent when Ellium used the term multiple times, followed by 'Phoenix.' Yes, Ellium was calling me 'Boy Phoenix' now.

I took another breath.

"Sorry to interrupt," I said loudly, "but I really need to get back to the scene. Regardless of what you may think of Rose, I have the fullest confidence in her. She is one of the best on the team."

It was obvious that the Directors were not fond of being interrupted, but I wasn't really worried about that. If they wanted to fire me, so be it.

"How will you replace the lost weapons?" Taragon asked.

"Excuse me?" I said, confused. "That's why I'm speaking to you."

"To us?" Taragon answered. "We don't have a stockpile of weapons for you. Besides, the Badlands PPD has a minimal budget."

"I noticed," I said, "but under the circumstances, we really—"

"Even with the budget he has," interrupted Ellium, "he could get a small stash of weapons underground."

Taragon's pixels moved up and down. "Valid suggestion, Ellium."

"I know."

I was having difficulty doing more than blinking in disbelief at the screen. Unless I was completely misreading things, a Director of the Paranormal Police

Department just intimated that it wouldn't be such a bad idea to buy a block of weapons from traffickers. To make matters worse, another of those Directors agreed with the suggestion.

"It isn't a bad idea," admitted Long.

And that made all three Directors raising their hands in favor of swapping PPD cash for mob weapons.

"Are you suggesting I buy weapons from the very criminals I'm supposed to be policing?" I asked, knowing damn well that's what they had meant.

Again, the pixels froze for a couple of seconds, after which Ellium said, "Uhhh…no?"

Sigh.

"What about Netherworld Proper?" I asked. "Isn't that who provides us with our regular shipments and such?"

"I don't think you understand the request, Chief Phoenix," Long said. "Netherworld Proper is some distance from the Badlands."

"Yes, I know," I replied. "While you may not know it by looking at me, I'm actually quite decent at reading a map. What I'm not great at, is navigating the bureaucracy well enough yet to get Netherworld Proper to send us an emergency shipment. That's where I need help."

"Impossible," Ellium said. "The next shipment of inventory, including armaments, won't be until next month."

"Hence the 'emergency shipment' piece of my argument."

"It can't be done," Long stated.

I gritted my teeth and stared at them. Yes, Hilda had warned me that this was going to be one of the most challenging positions I would ever hold, but she also warned me that failure would not go unpunished. Valkyrie punishments are of the terrifying sort, though, and I had no desire to face one.

"We won't last a month without weapons," I noted, soberly. That's when a thought struck. "Hey, wait. Okay, so you don't want to contact them and ask them to drive the cargo here, right?"

"Your powers of deduction are stunning, dragon," Ellium snarked.

"Better than that stupid hellion you had a few months back, Smellyum," Long said, coming to my defense.

"Did you dare just refer to me as 'Smellyum'?"

"If the filled-diaper fits—"

"Can I take a team and pick up the weapons cache?" I asked, loudly.

"You want to take a team to Netherworld Proper and convoy back a truckload of weapons?" Taragon asked. "Were you *in* the building during the blast?"

"No," I replied, confused.

"Have you received a head injury lately?" Long asked. "Did debris fall on you?"

"Maybe you tripped and knocked your skull on a steel beam?" added Ellium.

Ah. They were being facetious. Nice.

"What's the problem with my plan?" I asked, keeping my face cold.

"It's obtuse," Ellium said, quietly. "What you're suggesting is a suicide mission, Chief Phoenix. We can't, in good conscience, sanction something such as this."

"But you can, in good conscience, allow the Badlands

PPD to be completely wiped out because we don't have any weapons to defend ourselves?"

Silence from the monitors.

I had them on the ropes and I knew it. Still, I wasn't going to push them any further just yet. They clearly weren't stupid. Egotistical to the point of letting obvious solutions cloud their vision, absolutely...but not stupid.

"We can let you do this on one condition," Ellium spoke for the consortium. "You may only take volunteers. You may not order anyone to take this mission with you."

"I'll ask my team," I agreed. "Do we have vehicles? Trucks of some kind?"

"The Morgue has a fleet division," Long replied. "They have been known to allow the PPD to utilize its vehicles— at a reasonable rate. Deadhaul, I believe the service is called."

"Deadhaul? Really?"

"It's The Morgue," Long said. "What did you expect it to be called?"

"Not that."

"A few things you should know, Chief Phoenix," Taragon said.

This was where they washed their hands of me when the shit hit the fan, despite the fact that they were providing both: ample amounts of shit and industrial sized fans.

"You and your team are acting under NOC—Non-Official Cover. If you or any of your team are caught or killed, we will disavow any knowledge of your actions."

"Oh, good," I grunted. "It's not like this mission is impossible or anything."

"I'd watch my tone if I were you, Chief," Ellium said, "We are providing significant leeway in your undertaking of this mission. Is that understood?"

"Understood, sir," I said. "Do we have a contact in the Netherworld?"

"Chief Carter," Long answered. "I hear his wife runs Requisitions in his jurisdiction. We will alert him of your situation through non-official channels."

"Chief Carter, got it."

"Even if he agrees, and he may not," Long said, "you will be bringing weapons over the most inhospitable terrain in the Netherworld. They won't pass the neutral area. After the wall, you and your team are on your own. I suggest you get yourself an excellent lead driver."

"I believe I speak for all of us when I say good luck," Taragon said. "Remember, your team must not be coerced into this. Volunteers only."

"I understand."

I just needed to find a group of insane PPD officers willing to risk life and limb to travel across the Netherworld, bringing trucks full of weapons back into the Badlands, where every criminal will be waiting to ambush us.

Sounded like the perfect job for Alpha Team.

"That will be all for now, Chief," Taragon answered. "Be safe out there."

The monitors went dark, and the door behind me slid open.

When I stepped back into my office, Rose was waiting for me.

"We have an issue," she said, flexing the muscles of her jaw. "An issue *you* need to deal with—now."

She turned and walked out of my office before I had a chance to answer. We moved down the ruined corridors and turned into one of the semi-intact conference rooms. She opened the door and motioned for me to enter with a flourish.

I stepped inside and saw a woman standing in full battle armor, looking out of the shattered window. Another person, who looked like a young child, was sitting still in one of the chairs around the large center table. Rose stepped in behind me and shut the door.

"Mom?" I asked, completely lost. "What are you doing here? Even more importantly, what the hell is *he* doing here?"

"Hello, Ezekias," Hilda said as she turned to face me. "I told you to never call me that in public."

"Sorry," I replied. "Why are you two here?"

"I need a favor."

CHAPTER 7

*A*nyone who's seen a valkyrie, never forgets the image.

This woman towered above me by a good four inches. Her body was an example of what I would call the perfect physique. Every muscle was developed and chiseled. Her long blonde hair was tied in a braid that hung down to her waist. She defined strength and fierceness. Everything about her screamed 'I am a valkyrie. Displease me, and I will crush you without a second thought.'

Hilda defined what it meant to be a warrior. As leader of the Dragon's Teeth valkyries, it was her responsibility to train and fight alongside her army of warrior women.

There were a few sects of valkyries in the Badlands. This was because they all had differing opinions on how the valkyrie nation should be run. Hilda's style was strict and exacting, and she rarely changed her mind once a decision was made. To do so was a sign of weakness, as it proved a lack of forethought. Weakness was not tolerated in Hilda's valkyrie nation.

Today, it looked like Hilda was riding off into battle, dressed in full armor that glistened and reflected the light. Her battle armor kicked up the piss-your-pants intimidation by a factor of ten.

Even Rose gave her a healthy amount of distance. Hellions were machines of destruction, but no one—*no one* picked a fight with a valkyrie, because even if you won...it'd hurt.

"Did Ragnarok begin?" I asked. "I didn't get the memo."

She stepped close to me and slapped me hard across the face. Other mothers hugged their children, or so I was told. Not Hilda. Her slaps were her way of toughening us up.

"Valkyries don't hug," I remembered her answer when I asked her why she never hugged me. *"Not unless we're burying a sword into your midsection."*

Valkyrie parenting: not for the weak-hearted.

"You're looking good," she said, giving me the once over. "A bit scrawny though. You could stand to eat some more. I think I brought—"

She rummaged through a pack she carried. Flashbacks of her meals grabbed me by the throat, gut-punching me repeatedly.

"No!" I blurted. She gave me a sharp look in response. "I mean, no, thank you," I added, quickly tapping my midsection. "I had a large breakfast."

Her stare lingered for a moment.

"Why are you here, again?" I asked.

She glared at me for a second longer and then smiled. Some people have pleasant dispositions, which leads to pleasant facial expressions. Hilda wasn't one of them. Her face rebelled at the thought of a non-feral smile, which meant it defaulted to the smile she used right before punching a sword through an opponent's chest, excavating their still-beating heart, and having a light snack as they fell to the ground dying.

It was not a pleasant smile.

"I need a favor, son."

Uh oh.

"I'm kind of in the middle of a disaster," I answered, looking around. "In case you haven't noticed."

"Oh, I thought this was the usual decor?"

I shook my head.

"Well, it should be."

"What do you need, Hilda?" I asked. Again, she never approved of my calling her mom in public. Probably had something to do with my being male and a dragon. "Can it wait?"

"No, it can't," she answered, driving her enormous broadsword into the floor, point first. "I have ValCon starting in two days, and you have to watch your brother."

My stomach turned.

"Excuse me, what?"

The little boy at the table waved at me. I ignored him.

His name was Pear, and he was a colossal pain in my ass. He was also my little brother...kind of.

"But he's such a pain," I whined.

Yes, whined.

Being around Hilda reverted me to teenage angst in three seconds flat.

"Don't whine," she replied, her eyes flashing. "It is unbecoming of a warrior."

Rose was looking at me like I'd just shat my pants. From her perspective, I'd done just that.

Ugh.

"This is a bad time, Hilda," I said semi-defiantly. "I can't watch him right now. There's just too much going on, and I'm responsible here. You taught me to always put duty first, remember?"

Hilda approached. Thankfully, she left the sword buried in the floor.

"Did I stutter?" Hilda asked as she stepped close. Rose moved away from me. "To my recollection, I don't recall having a speech impediment."

"Get Aunt Inga or Aunt Frigga to watch him," I stated, trying to keep the whine out of my voice as I stood my ground. "I'm busy."

"Both of them are coming with me to ValCon," Hilda said. She then got an air about her. One of those motherly things where you just knew that something was amiss. "But you say you're too busy. I understand."

"Thank you, I'm glad you—"

"Too busy for the woman who raised you, who braved dragon-fever when you fell ill." She walked back to her sword. "Isn't it funny how I was never 'too busy' to feed you, clothe you, change your diaper."

"I never wore a diaper!"

"True," she agreed. "I meant that I helped you change your pants when you had your 'fear accidents'." She turned to face Rose. "Did he tell you about those?"

"Uhhh…" Rose replied with a gulp.

"Nearly every time he sparred," Hilda sighed. "I'd never

seen a boy whimper, cry, and mess his pants as much as little Zekie."

"Zekie?" Rose choked, clearly holding back a laugh.

Great.

"And did I complain?" Hilda asked, rhetorically. "Of course I did. It's the only proper way to toughen up a young person."

I wasn't embarrassed. I was mortified.

"Look, Hilda," I started, my voice almost a growl, "I appreciate everything you—"

"And when you were cut and bleeding," she added. "Who poured blood ale on the wound to disinfect it?"

"Wounds *you* inflicted," I grunted. "And let's not forget the intensive valkyrie training that even you said was more than the average dragon could be expected to handle."

"Aye, it is!" She gave me the once over. "Clearly. Still, it was training to prepare *you*, to make you the dragon you are today." She let out a long, time-to-make-you-feel-guilty breath. "But now...now you're too busy for me."

"I'm not too—"

"Who was there when your wings first showed, Zekie? Me!"

"Because you threw me off Heaven's Fang! 'Today you fly or die.' That sound familiar, Mom?"

Her eye twitched, but whatever. She was calling me Zekie, so I was going to call her Mom. Until she throat-punched me, anyway.

"Of course it does," Hilda answered, finally, sounding proud to have thrown me off the cliff. "It was the day you became a warrior. The day I *made* you a warrior. You faced death that day and emerged victorious...because of *me*."

She pounded a fist on her chest causing the armor to reverberate with a clang.

"I nearly died," I said, realizing I would never win this battle.

"But you didn't," she countered. "Because of that... because of *me*...you are the chief of the Badlands Paranormal Police Department."

"Yeah, thanks," I said with a heavy dose of sarcasm.

"Finally, some gratitude."

I glanced over at Pear as my shoulders dropped. There was no guilt that hit quite as hard as a valkyrie mother's guilt. It was brutal.

No matter what kind of argument I could cook up, she'd have a counter.

There was just no way to slip out of this.

Besides, there was no doubt going to come a time when I'd need her help. Too much shit was going down on the Strip for me to get through the next year unscathed. If it came to that, I'd need to have some leverage. That was the one thing about valkyries that they refused to change: honor.

If I didn't watch Pear, she could deny me; if I *did* watch him, though, then she'd be honor-bound to help me if I came calling. Well, technically, she *could* say that mothering me was more than enough, but I knew her better than that.

I had to suffer some today so that I could get help tomorrow.

That's how it worked.

"Fine, leave him," I said, fighting to keep the grit out of my voice. "I'll keep an eye on him until you get back."

She removed the sword from the floor. "Excellent," she said with her scary smile. "I was really hoping it didn't come to using my sword. I just had it cleaned."

"Considerate of you," I said. "How long is this ValCon thing going to be? I may have to take a trip."

"A trip?" she said, musing. "Well, Pear *is* nearly a century old." She seemed to be hedging at this point. That was always the case with Pear. If things got a little too hairy, Hilda would protect him. Me? Hell no. I got my ass kicked. But Pear was little. Vicious as fuck, but little. Hilda mothered and protected him like he was a rare jewel. He kind of was, truth be told, but in my estimation it was the type of jewel that was better off buried. "I suppose it's time he get out and see some of the world," she said with some effort. "Take him with you, but watch him carefully. ValCon should only be a week or so."

"A week?" I asked. "I have to watch him for a week?"

"Or so," she said, quickly. "This is the Centennial Event. Its a special year, and I'm on the planning and presenting committee."

"You're...on the planning committee?" I asked incredulously. "What are you going to present—how to remove a sword arm in five easy steps?"

"Actually," she said quietly, hefting her beast of a sword, "it can be done in two. Would you like a demonstration?"

The part of my brain that had temporarily become suicidal, ran away, leaving me with the voice of cold clarity. Do not challenge a valkyrie in any type of sword play. Even when said valkyrie is your mother. You are asking for a world of pain…and learning to use your opposite, and only remaining hand.

"No, thank you," I said, moving away. "Enjoy your time at ValCon."

"I intend to," she said. Then she looked over at my brother. "Mind your big brother, Pear."

"Yes, Mom."

See? Pear was allowed to call her 'mom' in public.

Fucker.

Hilda handed me a slender, metal rod on a chain

"Will I need this?" I said, placing the chain around my neck and letting the rod fall under my shirt.

"I sincerely hope not," she replied, giving one last look at Pear.

She was obviously conflicted about leaving him with me.

"He's your responsibility, Zekie," she stated evenly. "Do *not* disappoint me."

With that, she left the room, and I was able to breathe regularly again.

CHAPTER 8

"*H*e's cute," Rose said, looking at Pear. "Your mother, on the other hand...is...formidable."

"That's one way to describe her," I scoffed. "Sure. Let's go with that."

"So, is he a dragon, like you?" Rose asked, staring at Pear. "Why does he have fangs, claws, and pointy ears? He looks like a cute pixie."

"Pixie?" I asked with a wince. "Not seeing it. Fangs, claws, and pointy ears come with the package."

"Closer to that than what you are," she stared at his face. "He doesn't have your eyes, though. The rest...kind of makes sense."

"No, he doesn't," I said. "Be thankful."

"Can he unleash his full dragon?"

Pear was about half my height. Dark brown hair hung over his pointed ears. Every time he smiled, he flashed his pointed teeth in our direction with a grin of mischief.

"He's not a full dragon," I said. "He's half-dragon."

"Why does he smile like that?" she asked. "It looks like he's plotting something evil."

"That's probably because he is," I said. I then pointed at my brother. "Pear, no."

Pear had extended his claws and began raking them across the conference table, leaving deep grooves in the wood.

Rose raised an eyebrow.

"What's the other half?" Rose asked, admiring the scratches Pear left in the wood.

"Were-bear, he's a Bragon," I said, trying to change the subject. "We need to deal with our main situation, Rose."

"Rose?" Pear asked, looking up at Rose. "That's a pretty name. My big brother is pretty amazing. I have the best big brother."

"I thought he was older than you?" Rose asked under her breath as Pear began running around the room. "How are you the big brother?"

"I'm taller," I said with a sigh. "He means it literally. I'm physically the bigger brother."

"Ah," Rose said. "I've never heard of a bragon. Does he turn like you?"

"Something like that."

"Into a bear?"

"Not really," I said, remembering what Pear transformed into the last time he unleashed his second form. "Not exactly. Pear...Pear, sit down—now."

Pear continued running around the table for a few more circuits before parking himself in one of the chairs. He sat there beating the table lightly with his fingers to a rhythm only he could hear.

"What?" Rose asked. "Is the dragon half too strong?"

"It can be."

"Does he turn into a small dragon?"

"Not exactly, but kind of?" I then yelled, "Pear, no! Do not chew on the chairs!"

Rose gave me a look. "Don't you think you should be nicer to him? He *is* your brother."

"Ask me that again after you've spent more than a few minutes with him."

"I think he's adorable," she said, crossing her arms at me. "You're just jealous that he gets his mother's attention more than you do."

"Yeah, I'm sure that's it," I quipped. "Anyway, we need to focus on our current situation." She dropped her angst. "I spoke to the Directors."

"Yeah, I know," Rose said, still looking at Pear. "Are they going to send us the weapons?"

I told her what the Directors had said. Rightfully, she was getting angrier by the second.

"Rose," I said, slowly. "Take a breath."

"Take a breath?" she said, raising her voice. "Take a fucking breath?"

"Takeafuckingbreathtakeafuckingbreathtake-fuckingbreath!" Pear yelled from the chair, beating his hands in time with each word. "Take...a... fucking...breath!"

He beamed with the knowledge of a child who knew they had done something wrong, but fully owned it. It would almost have been adorable if he wasn't ninety-six years old.

I stared at Rose, who looked away, suppressing a laugh.

"Thank you for that, really," I said, glaring at Pear, who was still whispering the words under his breath. "Stop it, Pear."

"Do you want me to take a fucking breath?" Pear asked with a smile. "I can, you know."

"No, Pear," I said with a sigh. "I don't."

"Does he always do that...repeat what he hears?" Rose asked with an evil smile.

"Only the words you don't want him to—Rose," I said, raising a finger. "No."

"Well, shit," she said, leaning over the table and examining the gouge marks again. "This little fucker has some sharp claws."

"Wellshitlittlefucker!" Pear yelled. "Wellshitlittlefucker!"

Rose stared at him for a few moments in the middle of his proclamation.

"He's not too bright is he?" she asked, smiling. "The lights are on, but is anyone home?"

"There's a reason bragons are rare," I said. "They're reckless as hell and about as sharp as a tennis ball. They've even been known to charge an army of trolls."

"*One* bragon?" Rose said, looking at Pear with admiration. "Against an army?"

"It's a short battle," I noted. "Still, the bragon can hold his own until a troll introduces him to a fist, a club, or any variation of the two."

"That *is* impressive, and potentially fatal."

"No sense of danger, and once they turn, they're

virtually unstoppable."

She seemed to be weighing the situation. Maybe she'd back off on the adoration and get to the point where I was with Pear. Translation: he's a dangerous little bastard who is bound to bring nothing but trouble.

"He's still cute," Rose said.

So much for that.

"We're taking him with us, right?" she asked. "You're not going to try and leave him here, are you?"

"No choice," I said. "He can't be left with someone who doesn't understand him. That's why Hilda dumped him on me."

"Should *he* be watching *you?*" Rose questioned. "He's older than you are."

"And about as clever as a brick," I replied. "If I leave him alone, trust me, the damage is incalculable."

"That sounds perfect for this trip," Rose said. "He'll fit right in."

"Speaking of...we need to mobilize the team," I said. "And get a driver."

"I think I know where we can get a driver," Rose said. "My old offensive driving instructor, Bernard. He's retired, but he can still drive."

I squinted at her. "You mean defensive driving, right?"

"Have you seen me drive?" Rose asked. "Have I ever been defensive?"

"Good point."

"Offensive—the best defense is a good offense," Rose answered. "No such thing as defensive driving."

Doe appeared at the door to the conference room.

"We have a situation."

CHAPTER 9

*D*oe took in the scene and stepped back.

"What is that?" he asked, pointing at Pear. "More importantly, why is it here?"

"It's not a *what*," I said. "It's my little brother...kind of." Unless someone knew Pear's age, they would buy that he was my little brother, so it was probably best to just own it. Pear considered me his big brother anyway, so it wasn't like he'd contradict me. "Anyway, what's the situation?"

"We have Rouge Riders heading this way," Doe answered, checking his guns. "I don't know how word got out so fast, but they aren't coming here for lunch."

"Shit," hissed Rose.

"Rouge Riders?" I asked, looking at Rose. "What are Rouge Riders?"

"Follow me," Rose said, running out of the conference room. "I had a feeling something like this was going to happen."

I tried to hook the connector to the group, but it didn't work.

"*Group chat, Ro,*" I commanded the station AI.

A high-pitched whine came across the comms making me wince.

"*Enabled group chat is,*" Rowena answered. "*Disturbance in the signal there may be.*"

"*Listen up,*" Rose said, rubbing her ears. "*We have Rouges incoming. Get your asses to the station now. We need as much weaponry here as possible.*"

"*On our way,*" Silk and Butch answered. "*We're about twenty minutes out.*"

"*Graffon and Doe can cover the main entrance,*" Rose said. "*I need to brief the chief on the Riders. We'll cover the rear. Nimble, can you initiate a station lockdown?*"

"*Yes, I just need to get into my system,*" he answered. "*Tam and Yarrl can split up and assist main and rear entrances.*"

"*I call Tam,*" Rose said. "*You two can have Yarrl.*"

"Rouge Riders?" I asked aloud, following Rose to her locker. "Who are they?"

She pulled out a bag.

"I really hope you kept some of those shotgun rounds in the station," she said, looking through the bag. I counted at least twenty, fully-prepped speed loaders for her Smith & Wesson .500's hand-cannons—*Last Word* and *Lethal Mercy*. She zipped the bag closed and tightened the holsters holding the guns on either side of her body. "Yes or no?"

"*Pinky* and *Butterfly* are always ready to go," I stated, opening my jacket and showing off the sawed-off shotguns hanging in my modified shoulder holsters. "Dragon rounds and armor piercing are in my office and in the car. I'm carrying about fifty of each. The rest of the cache is at the Dirty Goblin."

"You couldn't find better names for those things?" Rose asked, nodding at my two lethal babies. "Those have to be the worse names for guns I've ever heard...really."

"That's the point," I answered. "Everyone wants to be taken down by the Last Word or Lethal Mercy. No one wants to be dropped by Pinky or Butterfly. The names are actually a deterrent to violence. Yours start a fight."

"Is there a reason you're keeping three hundred rounds of shotgun ammo at Percy's?"

"Did you forget my first day as Chief?" I asked, shaking my head. "Percy hasn't. With all the time I spend there, three hundred rounds may not be enough."

She snorted. "Is he still tetchy about the damage? The PPD only made him pay for half the construction cost. He got lucky."

Pear was tugging on my sleeve. I glanced down, giving him a sharp look. He rolled his eyes and sighed.

"I think he's over it," I answered Rose, finally. "The last time he mentioned it, I offered to have Graffon come over and explain things to him. Calmed him right down."

"Good," she said. "You still have the devastator?"

A while back, one of the Shumants had outfitted me with a hellion devastator. I pointed to the blade strapped to my thigh.

"Slice and Dice," I said. "Never leaves my side."

Pear reached for it.

I slapped his hand away.

He stuck his tongue out and ran back down the hall to

the conference room. He was definitely a variable I didn't need to deal with right now.

"If you run out of ammo," said Rose, "you'd better make sure it leaves your side, and buries itself in someone's chest."

She made sure her calf sheaths were tight. My devastator was a lethal blade designed and created by hellions. Her blades, Soulsplitter and Divisor, made Slice and Dice look like a butterknife.

Yes, I remembered the names of her weapons. Compared to the names of my weapons—her names were badass.

Not that I would ever tell her that.

We headed to the rear of the building and made a detour to the conference room where Pear was sitting quietly. Immediately I knew something was wrong. Pear never sat still for long, unless—I saw the chunk missing from the far end of the conference table. Rose raised an eyebrow at the damage and gave Pear a short nod.

"Stop destroying the furniture," I stated firmly, "and stay in here. I'm going to lock this door. Some bad people are coming."

Pear looked up with a smile reminiscent of Hilda and chilled my blood.

"Can I help?" he asked. "I'm very good with bad people...very good."

"No, not this time," I said with a shudder. "This time you stay here. Do you understand? Stay here."

I stepped back and locked the conference room door, watching him through the window.

Pear looked up, sniffed the air, and turned his head,

slowly letting a smile spread across his lips. Even after all these years, he managed to make my scales curl.

"That's not creepy at all," Rose said, stepping back. "What *exactly* is a bragon again? I mean…what happens when a dragon and a werebear mix?"

Creepy didn't begin to describe him. Everything about Pear was disturbing.

"Trust me, you don't want to know."

"Do you think he's going to stay in there?" she asked. "Will he listen to you?"

"For the most part, yes," I replied, even though I had my doubts. "But we better deal with these Rouge Riders soon." My hackles were up. "If he transforms, Rouge Riders will be the least of our worries."

CHAPTER 10

"Who are these Rouge Riders?" I asked. "And give me the short version."

"They're not really Rouge as in red," Rose said. "It's really the Rogue Riders."

"What?" I asked, confused. "Then why call themselves the Rouge Riders?"

"Back when they were forming the group, they called themselves the Rogue Riders. Someone had stationery, business cards, even the organizational sign made up."

"Strange, but I don't see the issue."

"Whoever made up all of the signage and stationery, misspelled Rogue with Rouge."

"Wouldn't it be easier just to change the name—?"

"Jackets, headquarters signage, business cards, vehicles, everywhere they were the Rouge Riders," Rose said, stifling a laugh. "To change all of that would be to admit they made a mistake."

"Still not seeing—"

"Out there, admitting a mistake like that?" Rose said,

shaking her head. "May as well hang it up and call it a day. They would be seen as weak, indecisive targets."

"So they kept Rouge Riders," I said slowly, "because that would clearly be a *strong* decision? Seriously?"

"Seriously, the Rouge Riders are castoffs from the Company and other assorted criminal organizations." Rose was heading to the rear entrance. "They were thrown out or forced out. Most of them are disgruntled or banned malkyries."

"And now what?" I asked. "They only wear red?"

"I'll get to that in a second," she said. "The leader of the Riders is Sal, a malkyrie who was banned from his clan."

"Not Butch's—?"

"No," Rose answered. "A sister clan to Butch's."

"Sister?"

"Wait until you see them. Anyway, malkyries are similar to valkyries in that they will join forces to face a common enemy, but usually exist in small clans in times of peace."

"I think I know where this is headed," I said, nodding my head. "So, what? They take down the PPD and they get credibility with the other organizations?"

"No one likes the PPD," Rose said, making sure her guns were locked and loaded. "At least none of the criminals."

"Same goes for the Houses," I said. "Hellions and dragons aren't fans either."

"Like I said," Rose answered, peeking out one of the windows, "none of the criminals."

"How many of these Riders are we talking about?" I

asked, trying to calculate my ammo. "How are they outfitted?"

"These guys are the bottom of the barrel," Rose answered. "That means they have the largest number of incompetent thugs. They have a good amount of malkyries, and then a mix of everything."

"Should be easy then," I said. "We shoot to wound and restrain them."

"No," Rose said her voice hard. "We only need to take down the leader and they should scatter."

"That makes it easier."

"And harder," she answered. "You forget the part where he's a malkyrie?"

She was right, of course, but she was also forgetting how I was raised.

There was a certain way to handle valkyries. Typically, it was through groveling and begging, but sometimes just standing up to them and giving it everything you had was enough to change their view of you. If your fight was just, the willingness to put your life on the line for your beliefs revealed honor…assuming your beliefs weren't idiotic, of course.

"Let me deal with this," I said. "I have some experience with valkyries, as you may recall."

"Which means nothing with malkyries," Rose replied.

Again, correct. The clan where I was raised was purely female, except for me and Pear, obviously, but we weren't malkyries either.

"Our best chance is holding them off until Butch gets here," Rose added.

I sighed. It sucked sitting around when you had a job to do.

With a grunt, I said, "You didn't explain what they do to make the Rouge Riders moniker fit."

"I know," Rose said. "It's hard to put in words. Better if you experience it."

"This sounds suspiciously like the funeral party hazing," I said, warily. "What aren't you telling me?"

"What makes you think I would keep anything from you?" Rose answered with a slight smile. "You're the chief. It's better if you're informed. That way, when you go down, at least you'll know why."

I frowned at her. "Not feeling filled with confidence here."

"Each gang has its own look, right?"

"I have no idea."

"Well, you do now, and the Rouge Riders are just like the rest of the gangs in that they have their own look," Rose stated. "They have to be experienced—trust me. They may be a hodgepodge group of misfits, but they're led—"

"Led by a malkyrie," I interrupted, looking outside. "I get it."

"And that makes them a threat not to be taken lightly."

I was clearly not going to get any further details from Rose, and that was fine. I'd learn sooner rather than later what the Rouge Riders bit was all about. I had my suspicions, but with everything I'd seen since landing on the Strip, I decided it best to squelch my thoughts until the truth was revealed.

"Everyone ready?" I asked over the comms. Everyone acknowledged. Good. *"Butch, how far out are you?"*

"Butch is about as far out as you can get," Silk answered quickly with a laugh.

"Hilarious," I said. *"What's your ETA, Butch? Rose tells me you're our best chance of dealing with the Rider leader."*

"Best chance?" Butch shot back. *"When I see that bitch I'm going to put my foot so far up his ass he's going to taste my toes."*

Silk erupted in laughter.

"That's one visual I can't erase," I muttered under my breath and looked at Rose. "Best chance? Really?"

"Apparently they aren't on speaking terms any longer," Rose said with a shrug. "Who knew?"

"Silk and Butch incoming on the front approach," Doe announced. A few seconds later, he added, *"They're in the station, Chief. We also have several dozen of the Riders. Means the rest will try the rear approach."*

"Don't they always?" Silk asked followed by another eruption of laughter and gasps. *"Sorry, Butch. No...no offense."*

"None taken," Butch replied, his voice on edge. *"We're taking positions on the front entrance. You let me know when Sal shows up so I can introduce his face to my fist. Last time I lend him my favorite pair of Frisian Bouloutins, I'll tell you that."*

"He hates this Sal over a pair of shoes?" I asked Rose, aloud. "Is he serious?"

Rose raised an eyebrow. "I'm surprised you know what they are."

"I may have been raised in a cave, but I was brought up by women. I know they're shoes of some kind."

"They're not just *any* pair of shoes," Rose answered, drawing her guns. "Combat Bouloutins are an experience. Anyone fortunate enough to own a pair of blue bottom boots—it's a matter of status. Rouge Riders wear the most expensive combat footwear in the Badlands, available only to malkyries."

"Do you own a pair?"

"That's like asking if I have scales," Rose snapped. "I'm not a malkyrie."

"That's not an answer."

"I'm a hellion, Chief," she said, glaring at me. "Even though I could probably kill anything, even while wearing heels, regular combat boots are better suited for my chosen line of work. I wouldn't invest in a pair of those overpriced status symbols."

She'd proven that fact time and again. Still, something told me that there were times when Rose wasn't donning combat boots. She looked like she would clean up quite nicely, if she put her mind to it.

That wasn't exactly a grand vision to think about, though. A fashionable Rose would probably be even more lethal.

Shudder.

"*What did this Sal do?*" I asked through the connector, pushing the image of Rose wearing a dress out of my head. "*Did he scuff those boots or something?*"

"*He damaged the soles,*" Butch huffed. "*Then had the audacity to say it was my fault because I was too heavy.*"

I looked the question at Rose.

Rose shook her head. "I'd shoot him just for calling me fat," she said. "Damaging a pair of Combat Bouloutins deserves pain with a side of maiming."

"You have to be fucking kidding," I said. "Damaged the soles? How do you avoid that while wearing them?"

"Seriously, Chief, in the malkyrie community, ruining a pair of Bouloutins is a serious issue."

"How serious?" I asked. "Serious enough to kill?"

"Malkyries *are* vigorously passionate about their fashion, but I don't know if they would kill for it. Crazier things have happened, though."

The sound of movement was just outside, signaling that the Rouge Riders were indeed on their way in.

"I heard you ruined a pair of Bouloutins, Sal," I yelled. "I understand this is serious in the malkyrie community. How about we make a deal?"

"A deal?" Rose hissed. "What are you doing?"

"That bitch Butch has been flapping his lips, I see," Sal replied. "If he weren't so fat—excuse me, slightly overweight—the soles would've lasted longer! I almost broke an ankle! Fuck that! Kill everyone!"

"Guess he's as sensitive about the whole broken sole incident as Butch, eh?"

"You had to bring it up?" Rose asked, returning fire. "What were you going to offer him...a new pair of Bouloutins?"

"Something like that," I said, sliding behind a wall as gunfire raked where I was hiding a second earlier. I could hear footsteps on the floor above us. I hoped they wouldn't open the conference room door. "They can't be *that* expensive."

"You really have led a sheltered life," Rose said before rolling across the floor and emptying one of her hand cannons, destroying one of their vehicles. "You can't even get them if you're not a malkyrie."

Gunfire erupted around the rear door.

"Come on out, Chief," Sal yelled. "I promise not to kill you right away."

"That sounded creepy," I whispered to Rose.

She nodded. "Still want to shoot to wound?"

"We aren't criminals," I reaffirmed. "Incapacitate them with extreme pain if necessary, but don't kill them. I want to find out how they knew about our current status."

I took a breath.

"So, Sal," I called out again after more gunfire erupted around the door, "to what do I owe the pleasure of your visit?"

"You're our ticket to becoming legit," he answered. "We take care of you, everyone has to respect us, and then maybe we can get all of our stationary redone and take off this ridiculous makeup."

I peeked out and noticed that all of the men with Sal wore black leather jackets with their group name embroidered in bright red letters that misspelled Rogue, and they had on some hideously bright red combat boots. The whole ensemble was finished off with equally red bandannas. And there was that makeup. It did look a little strange, especially on the ones who sported beards and mustaches.

Plus, I noticed they were mostly malkyries, or at least built like them.

"I thought you said they were all races?"

"They are," Rose answered. "The majority of them are malkyries, but they'll accept anyone as long as you like red and are okay putting on rouge."

"Right," I muttered, ducking back behind the door frame. "Those...are really red boots."

"They had to embrace the Rouge Riders somehow," Rose said.

"You mean besides the makeup?"

"It does look a little strange on them" she replied with a nod, "especially the ones with the beards and mustaches."

"A little bit."

"Like I said, Chief, they take mistakes seriously down here."

I gave her a look, but called out, "Killing us won't earn you respect, Sal. Why not leave now, before someone gets hurt?"

"Actually, Chief, yes it will," Sal replied. "I'm going to shoot you right after I take care of Butch."

I raised a sarcastic eyebrow at Rose. "That's kind of him."

"Don't bother with the doors," Sal yelled to the men. "This place is full of holes. They can't cover them all. Get inside and bring them out. Keep the Chief alive...for now."

I heard footsteps as the Riders entered the station. Some of them bypassed us and went upstairs. A few of them tried to flank us, but Rose convinced them it was a bad idea with her guns.

"Sal, don't make me shoot you," Rose said, blasting holes in some of the cars. "Call your men off and walk away."

"Walk away?" Sal answered with a laugh. "Girl, we are the first of many. Everyone on the Strip knows the PPD is short on hardware. You have no weapons and we have plenty. *We're* going to walk away—but you aren't."

"What does he mean by 'everyone'?"

"Exactly what it sounds like, I'd guess," Rose said, exchanging rounds. "Word is out on the street, we're unarmed. You thought the funeral party was bad? This is going to make that look like a good day at the office."

Screams erupted from upstairs.

"Shit," I said, moving to the stairs with Rose in tow. "That doesn't sound good."

CHAPTER 11

"*N*imble," I said over the comms, *"did you get access to the lockdown sequence?"*

"Yes, Chief," Nimble answered. *"It was a bit complicated. I had to run a subroutine, and then use a backdoor I had installed, but—"*

"Sounds fascinating," I said quickly. *"Initiate the lockdown. Now."*

"While we're still inside?"

"While we're still breathing," I replied. *"A condition I'm sure you'd like to maintain."*

"I have grown fond of breathing," Nimble answered *"You do realize that some gastropods—"*

"Nimble," Rose said, cutting him off, *"can you save the biology lesson for later and close the station down. Now!"*

"Of course," Nimble answered, flustered. *"Initiating lockdown sequence."*

Steel panels slid slowly over the doors and windows, sealing off all entrances and exits. The panels were covered in symbols that gave off a subtle orange glow.

"What are those?" I asked, pointing.

"Wards," Rose answered. "Mages put them there to offer extra protection. That's the reason these panels are moving so damn slow. It's giving them time to charge to full strength."

"How long does the lockdown sequence take?" I asked watching the panels creep down on tracks. *"At this rate, we'll be dead before they fully close."* The panels inched along like a snail crossing gravel. *"Seriously, can this sequence move any slower? That was a rhetorical question, Nimble."*

"Understood," Nimble answered. *"The sequence will be completed in ten minutes. It was designed to give everyone a chance to get safe. Can't have warded steel panels slamming down everywhere. Imagine the casualties."*

"We're going to be casualties if we don't get out of here," I said.

Rose and I slipped around the corner as soon as there was enough cover. We headed upstairs to the sound of more screams filling the corridors.

"Is that—?" Rose asked as we ran down the corridor. We stopped around the corner from the conference room. "What?"

"Someone opened the door to the conference room," I said, holding out my arm to prevent Rose from proceeding. "Don't get too close. I'm serious."

"It's your little brother," Rose said, pointing past my arm. "Are you going to leave him to the Riders?"

"It's not Pear I'm worried about," I said, keeping my voice low. "Whoever opened that door is gone. I'm worried about *us*."

"Gone?" Rose asked, incredulously. "What do you mean, gone?"

"As in, Pear dealt with them." I gave her a look. "Don't make any noise."

"Really," Rose scoffed. "How dangerous can a cute little bragon be?"

A pair of shredded, bloody, red boots sailed down the corridor past us. The beating of flapping wings filled the space, followed by a long scratching sound.

"That answer your question?" I asked. "Don't make any sudden moves."

"Shit," Rose said, serious. "Where's the rest of him?"

"He's probably all over the conference room," I said. "Those boots are probably the only thing still left in mostly one piece."

"You initiated a lockdown with that *thing* in here with us?" Rose hissed. "Are you insane?"

"That *thing* is my brother, as you may recall?"

"No offense, but most dragons are dangerous, uncontrollable, mindless beasts. Werebears are typically better, but when they go full bear...not so much." She glanced at the bloodied boots. "Mixing them together is obviously a bad idea."

"Now you're getting it," I agreed. "As for that dig about dragons, tell me again how hellions are made?"

"Fuck you," Rose said. "We are efficient engines of destruction, but we aren't mindless." She stared down the corridor. "Anyway, how do you plan on getting out of here with the lockdown in effect?"

"I studied the building plans," I said, and then opened a

channel. *"Nimble, how do we access the emergency exit once the building is on lockdown?"*

"Emergency exit?" Rose asked before Nimble could reply. *"Wouldn't that defeat the whole purpose of the lockdown? There's no—"*

"Actually the purpose of the lockdown is to keep whatever is outside...outside," Nimble said. *"For a PPD station, it would be prudent to have a method of egress, even during a lockdown."*

"We're going to need to get out of here," I stated. *"If these Riders are the first of many, I want Alpha Team out of the station and on the way to getting weapons."*

"I will send Tam to collect you and lead you to the exit," Nimble affirmed. *"It can be... complicated."*

"Good."

"Can't we just leave the rest of the Riders that made it inside to your brother?" Rose asked, looking at the boots. "It'd be faster than dealing with them ourselves."

"No," I said, glaring at her. "We need to calm him down."

"*We?*" Rose asked. "He's *your* little brother."

A roar tore through the corridor. I reached under my shirt and pulled out the small metal rod hanging from the chain Hilda had given me.

"What is that supposed to do?" Rose asked. "Is that a bragon controller or something?"

"It's a dragon whistle."

"A dragon whistle?" she screeched. "You feel we need *more* dragons on the scene?"

"This will calm the dragon side of him," I said. "Hilda always kept it close in case he got out of control. It should work." I licked my lips. "Hopefully."

"Hopefully?" Rose rasped. "Hopefully doesn't sound good. And what about you? What will that whistle do to you?"

"Nothing, I'm a full dragon. It will have no effect on me. It works on Pear because he's not purebred. I think."

"You're not sure? Have you used it before?"

"Not really, no."

"Wonderful," Rose said, throwing up a hand. "If you go psychodragon, I'm going to shoot you and call it a day."

"Your bullets can penetrate dragon scales?"

Rose looked at her guns, shaking her head. "Probably not, but my fists can."

I heard more voices from the other side of the corridor.

More Riders.

"Sal said to grab the chief," one of the voices noted. "We can erase anyone else."

"Ugh, the dust in here is clogging my pores," another voice said. "I'm going to need a full treatment at Lulu's when this job is done. Let's just find them, shoot them, and go. My skin is getting drier by the second, Brett."

"Shut it," Brett said. "We have a job to do, and in case you haven't noticed, this place is locked down, Ethan."

"What's that?" Ethan asked. "Is that a…little boy?"

"Have you been using that cheap brand of rouge again?" Brett asked. "I told you it has a high chemical content, and that it messes with your sensitive brain."

"I'm not imagining things," Ethan said, fear creeping into his voice. "That looks like a little boy…who had seriously ugly parents."

"Oh, wow, he looks a little more like a deformed troll, wouldn't you say?"

"That's quite possible," replied Ethan.

That's when I heard the devious cackling that only Pear could muster. It was a mix of giddy and disturbing, equaling a full-on evilness that made one's asshole pucker.

"What in the nine levels is that?" Brett shrieked. "Shoot it!"

Another roar sounded. This one was louder and longer than the first one and then...silence.

"Stay here," I commanded Rose, and then stopped and gave her a look. "If this doesn't work, find Tam and get the team out of here."

"What about you?"

"I'll probably have my hands full."

CHAPTER 12

I stepped around the corner and into the corridor.

The two Riders were still alive…barely. Pear had made quick work of them. For a half-dragon, he was completely frightening.

Pear had his wings out, his skin was covered in short, dense fur, and his face had transformed into some kind of animal with a long snout and a mouth full of long, razor-sharp fangs. His bloody hands sported claws that left grooves on every surface they grazed.

I blew the whistle and saw him turn slowly.

Non-dragons couldn't hear the noise it made. For me, it was a high-pitched sound, impossible to ignore, that cut through everything. Pear focused on me, but his eyes were vacant. It was like Rose said: the lights were on, but Pear was only partially there. He was in full-bragon mode. Good for him…bad for me.

"Hello, Pear," I said, raising my hands slowly. I learned long ago that sudden movements were understood as threats when he was in this mode. "It's me, your big brother."

Hilda never used the whistle. She would just make a fist and smash it into Pear's head until he calmed down. Valkyrie parenting wasn't known for being gentle and nurturing. I suppose the fact that she hadn't used her sword was a way of her showing restraint.

Pear snarled at me and I prepared to transform, just in case he felt I looked better in small pieces. I kept my gaze wide and approached slowly, keeping my hands raised. The two Riders on the floor were beat up and slightly mangled, but still alive.

"Relax, Pear," I said in a soothing voice. "It's me, ZeeZee. Remember?"

I heard a chuckle from around the corner and knew there would be no end to the comments from the team once Rose shared that nugget of information. As if Zekie wasn't bad enough.

When Pear first came to live with us, language had been a challenge. He couldn't form the complex sounds of my name and shortened it to the most pronounced sound...zee. My name transformed from Ezekias to ZeeZee and stayed there. In Pear's mind, it was easy and familiar. Bragons weren't overly intelligent, but they were fiercely loyal and highly intuitive. I was hoping that intuition would kick in now.

Pear shook the semi-conscious Rider, Brett or Ethan. Honestly, I didn't know which was which. They were both in bad shape. Pear gave me another grin. It was a grin that said 'new target with a side of fresh meat' acquired.

I blew the whistle harder.

He paused.

"ZeeZee?" he asked, cocking his head to one side and squinting as if looking into a bright light. "ZeeZee?"

"That's right," I replied, keeping my voice low and modulated. "It's me. Can you drop the Rider now? He looks just about done."

Pear turned to the Rider in his hand with mild surprise and dropped him with a thud. His wings, overly large fangs, and claws disappeared. The fur covering his body reverted back to skin, and he looked like a little boy again.

"I did it again, didn't I?" Pear asked, wiping his hand on the wall. "How many this time?"

"Well"—I looked at the blood-stained windows of the conference room—"one Rider for sure, and these two look like they were on their way to a final makeover."

For a short while after turning back, Pear exhibited high intelligence, and a fair amount of guilt. I had a feeling it was a result of the chemical dump that accompanied his transformation. The one time Hilda took him to have it tested, he reverted to his second form the moment a brave doctor buried a needle in his arm.

He introduced the medics to the concept of rapid evisceration as he shredded a room of doctors who wanted to experiment on the 'fascinating child' without strapping him down and sedating him first.

Only Hilda was able to calm him, giving a new definition to 'tough love' as she slammed the bragon forcefully out of his second form, and back into a little boy.

After that, she had the whistle made.

"Were they coming to injure you?" Pear said, looking around at the damage. "They don't look very friendly."

"You could say that," I said. "They were planning on killing my team, leaving me for last."

"Really?" he asked, and I could hear the anger rise in his voice. "Then maybe—"

"No," I said quickly. "You've done enough. It's going to take forever to get the Rider bits out of the conference room as it is. Besides, we need to go. More unfriendlies are coming, and we need to be gone by the time they get here."

"If that's the case," Pear said, "it would be in our best interest to vacate the premises. Especially if we are faced with an overwhelming criminal force."

It was so odd to hear him speak coherently.

"My thoughts exactly."

I grabbed him by the hand and pulled him back around the corner to a surprised Rose and Tam.

"He did this?" Tam asked, surveying the carnage in the conference room. "By himself?"

"I know, right?" Rose said with a smile and a nod. "Brutally impressive."

"Indeed," Tam answered. "He could prove to be quite useful."

They both seemed strangely pleased. Must've been a hellion thing.

"*Nimble,*" I commanded through the connector, "*have Tam and Yarrl neutralize any of the Riders trapped in the station after we leave. Just to be clear, neutralize doesn't mean eliminate, maim, or kill. Keep them in the holding cells...alive.*"

"Understood," Nimble replied. *"The sequence is complete. I can open the emergency exit once you get in position. Tam has assembled the rest of the team, and they're waiting for you downstairs. The Morgue has been instructed to await your arrival...alive, in this case."*

"What do you mean—in this case?"

"Francis is very pragmatic," Nimble answered. *"He wanted to know if you were arriving of your own volition, or if you were being delivered."*

"That's not morbid at all."

"I explained the situation, and he will have vehicles waiting for you at his premises. Note that we had to pay a considerable security deposit."

"Excuse me? Why?"

"You're heading into the neutral area to pick up weapons," Nimble answered. *"Then you're driving them back through some of the most hostile territory between here and the Netherworld."*

"So?"

"So their vehicles aren't cheap, Chief."

"They have no faith we'll return with the weapons," I mused.

"I have a better chance of completing a four-minute mile than you and your team returning, Chief," Nimble replied.

"You mean with the weapons? Right?"

"No, just returning at all, Chief."

CHAPTER 13

"Where is Lieutenant Bradley?" I asked as we moved down the corridor past my office, behind Tam. "He was supposed to come to my office."

"Right here, sir!" Bradley said from across the corridor. "You wanted to see me, sir?"

He was tall, for a goblin, and looked like he spent time in the station gym. His PPD uniform was ripped and dirty in several places, but I could tell he took pride in his appearance.

"Walk with me," I commanded as we kept pace with Tam. "The station is on lockdown. We have a few Rogues—"

"Rouges," corrected Rose.

"Right, that," I breathed. "Anyway, half our squad has been injured, and we're going to need more numbers."

"Sir?" Bradley asked, looking confused.

"While Alpha Team is on the road, doing our damnedest to get some weapons and ammo back here, you're in charge. I want you to tap into our officer recruitment pool at the Academy and get some new recruits in here, pronto."

"Yes, sir," Bradley answered, smartly. He pulled out his datapad. "It looks like we're currently at fifty percent operational. I have your authorization to bring that to one-hundred percent?"

"Absolutely," I confirmed. "I'm trusting you with this process. When I get back with the weapons, I want us at full strength, understood?"

"Understood, sir. May I ask where we're getting weapons? The armory is slagged, and, we're not due a shipment for another month at least."

"I can't say much, but we may have to go to Netherworld Proper," I said. "At the very least—to the neutral zone."

"Netherworld Proper?" he rasped. "To the neutral zone? That's risky."

"So I hear," I said. "Too bad we don't have much of a choice. If the Rouge Riders knew about our current status, that means other criminals know also. We have to get weapons fast."

"Sir, I have to officially voice my objection to this course of action," Bradley noted. "It's too dangerous for a small team. I'd advise you to take some officers from the station."

"You can't spare them," I declined as we got to the stairwell leading down. "Thanks for the suggestion, and the concern. Let's get our numbers back up. Nimble, Tam, and Yarrl will be on site to help you if you need them."

"Understood, sir," Bradley said with a salute. "Thank you for trusting me with this, sir. I won't let you down."

"We'll be back as soon as possible with a full contingent of weapons," I said, placing a hand on his shoulder. "In the meantime, keep the station locked down. Coordinate with Nimble regarding the rations and supplies. The station is self-contained and can be locked down for a month...maybe more since we're at fifty percent."

"Everything will be kept under control, sir," Bradley answered. "Good luck getting those weapons."

"Thanks," I said. "Oh, and grab some of the officers and round up the remaining Riders. Put them in the holding cells until I get back. No killing, unless absolutely necessary."

"Consider it done, sir," Bradley said. "Be safe out there, Chief. By the time you get back, we'll be at full strength again."

I headed downstairs behind Tam and Rose.

"I like that Lieutenant's energy," I said when I caught up to them. "Seems like he wants to do a good job."

"You know, if we don't make it back," Rose said. "He becomes the next Chief. A denizen of hell is next in line."

"You don't think—?"

"No, that would be you who doesn't think," she interrupted. "I trust Bradley about as much as I trust any goblin, which is not at all."

We reached the lower level. The corridor leading to the lab had been cordoned off.

Beyond it, I could see the destruction caused by the explosion. Some of the walls were destroyed, parts of the floor were missing. A low groan followed by creaking made it sound like the building itself was in pain.

"Is that area safe?" I asked as we headed in the opposite direction. "It sounds like it's going to cave in any second."

"No, it's not safe," Tam answered. "Fortunately, we are not going beyond the cordon. This way, please."

We headed down a few more dimly lit hallways until we reached a dead end. At the end of this corridor sat an impressive vault door and the rest of my team.

There was a chorus of, "Hello, Chief," followed by stares and silence when they saw the bloody mess that was my little brother. "What happened?"

"This is the chief's brother, Pear, and he's a genuine badass," Rose said, her voice hard. "Let's leave it at that and focus on what we need to do."

Rose briefed them.

"If any of you feel like this is too much or too dangerous, I'll understand if you want to stay," I announced. "Just say the word."

No one spoke.

"Sounds like a road trip!" Silk yelled, pumping an arm. "Let's roll out!"

I smiled.

My team may have been made up of misfits, but they were *my* misfits.

"Now that everyone's ready," I said, looking at Tam, "where does this exit lead? I didn't see that on the plans."

"That was a deliberate omission," Tam replied. "This exit will open into a tunnel. At the end of the tunnel, you will find several vehicles. Those vehicles have been prepped for immediate use—I suggest you take advantage of that, and leave the station with haste."

She walked over to a wall several meters away from the massive vault door.

"This door is biometrical," she pointed out, placing her hand on a section and revealing a recessed panel. "Once it's sealed from this side, only the Chief will be able to open it from the other side. Anyone else who tries, will trigger the failsafe." Her eyes grew stern. "Do not trigger the failsafe."

An orange horizontal line of energy scanned Tam's hand and disappeared. A section of the wall moved back and slid to the side. Rose led the team down the corridor. I stayed back to bring up the rear.

"Rose was following up on the delivery of the trigger," I said. "See if you can uncover who sent it."

"I will make sure to inform Nimble," Tam affirmed. "Whoever delivered the trigger may have a connection to the early Empiric delivery as well."

With a nod, I said, "I was thinking the same thing. If we can find out who sent the first delivery, we may also find who sent the second."

"Your logic is flawed, but the connection likely exists," Tam answered. "I will make sure we continue the investigation."

"Out of curiosity, what happens if you try that door?" I said, pointing at the massive vault door. "Where does that lead?"

"If you try that door," Tam said, glancing at the imposing structure, "it will lead to one place."

"Where?"

"Death."

*a*t the end of the tunnel we found ourselves in a small, underground parking facility.

"This isn't the station garage," Doe said, looking around. "This is an entirely different location."

"Did you know about this place?" I asked Rose as we all looked around. "Seems fairly new."

"No," she answered, heading to one of the three vehicles parked across the floor. They were some kind of cross-vehicle, not quite a car and not really a truck. Each of the black ones were covered with what appeared to be, armor plating. "Then again, we've never had a chief who exploded all the station's weapons, forcing us to evacuate before every criminal in Infernal City dusted our asses either. So, there's always a first time. Now, this...this is a sweet ride."

"I didn't explode all the station's weapons," I said defensively, walking over to the vehicle Rose had entered. "The package was sent to the station, and you know it."

Rose sat in the driver's seat and looked around.

"Addressed to you," she noted, poking her head out of her vehicle. "I don't see keys. Anyone see keys?"

I noticed the team paired off naturally—Doe with Graffon, Butch and Silk, and no one with Rose. They all glanced my way and shook their heads as I approached Rose's vehicle. Apparently, no one was suicidal enough to get in a vehicle with Rose...except me. Pear got in the back seat and bounced around until I stared at him. Then he bounced around and started humming simultaneously.

Great, his intellect had returned to 'normal.'

"Is he going to do that the whole time?" Rose asked, still looking for keys.

"Probably," I answered with a slight smile. "Isn't he adorable? Just wait, he gets even better."

"How the hell do we start these things?" Rose said and flexed her jaw. "Is Nimble deliberately trying to piss me off?"

I remembered what Tam had said about the door being biometric.

"Try letting it scan your hand," I said, pointing at the dashboard. "That panel over there maybe?"

"Biometric?" Rose scoffed. "PPD can't afford biometric ignitions. I'm still wondering where the money came from for this facility."

I placed my hand on the panel and the engine roared to life. After a few moments the other two vehicles came to life also.

"We need to get Bernard," Rose reminded me. "I should call him first, though. He's known to get a bit...cranky."

"Cranky?"

"He's old and tired," she waved at me. "Plus, he's a hellion."

"Is that why you're so cheerful all the time?" I asked. "This is a hellion thing?"

"This is about as happy and sociable as I'm ever going to be," Rose answered. "It's all downhill from here."

"Fantastic," I said. "I'm really looking forward to things getting even more abrasive." After a sigh, I asked, "Where is this Bernard?"

"I can tell you once we get out of here, but I have to call him first."

"He doesn't like guests?" I asked. "I've never heard of an introverted hellion."

"Bernie isn't introverted," she replied. "He's antisocial. We show up unannounced, he'll open fire on us the moment we step on his property."

"Sounds like a hellion," I muttered as she headed for the exit. "Can we avoid getting shot at for a few hours at least?"

She removed a PPD encrypted phone from her pocket and pressed a button, placing the call on speaker.

"Who needs to die?" answered the gruff voice, once the line connected. "You have five seconds...speak."

"Bernie, it's me," Rose said. "I have a job for you."

"Thorny?" Bernard asked. "That you? Well, fuck me sideways!"

"Call me that again and I'll shove one of my guns where it hurts and fire."

Bernard chuckled. "Pleasant as ever, I see," he said. "Still driving like your ass is on fire?"

"I learned from the worst."

"You learned from the only hellion crazy enough to get into a car with you. Every other instructor wasn't in the mood to die, mangled to a bloody pulp, after a fiery crash."

"Bernie?"

"Thorny?"

"Fuck you."

"Right," he said with a short laugh and grew serious. "What's the job?"

Rose briefed him, and he whistled.

"I see. *This* is the job where we *all* die in a fiery crash—transporting weapons for the PPD."

"Something like that," Rose said. "You in?"

"Hell yeah," Bernie answered. "Sounds like it will be a smooth ride."

Rose glanced into the rear-view mirror as we hit the street.

"Unlikely," she said and accelerated, sending out a quick connector call. *"Everyone stay tight on me. We have hostiles on our six."*

"When do I need to be ready?" Bernie asked.

"Now," Rose answered. "Pack light and bring hardware."

CHAPTER 15

"*W*ord travels fast in the Badlands," I said, looking behind us and picking up the two black vans who were pursuing us. "Are those Rouge Riders?"

"No," Rose said, swerving around traffic and cursing. "This thing has a fat ass. Riders won't leave the station, even if Sal is pissed at Butch. They will do everything possible to pull out their trapped members."

"Phrasing," I said under my breath. "Then who's after us and why? We don't have any weapons."

"But we're on our way to get some," Rose answered. "Those vans look like the Accountants."

"Accountants?" I asked, craning my neck to look behind us. "They want to discuss budgets?"

"They started out as legitimate accountants to criminals," Rose answered, nudging the vehicle between two cars.

This prompted a series of curses from Silk on the comms as he stayed right behind us.

"What happened?" I asked. "How did they go from accounting to criminals?"

"Accounting is a boring occupation, and they wanted to do something exciting," Rose said. "They went from skimming, to hostile takeovers of smaller organizations, to becoming a mid-range organization themselves."

"And they're after us because?"

"What part of 'everyone hates the PPD' did you not understand?" Rose snapped, stepping on the accelerator. "If any of these groups manages to take us out, the Badlands is done. We are the only line of defense against lawlessness in this city."

"That's a pretty thin line."

"No shit, Captain Obvious." Rose cut off three cars, veered into the left lane, and then swerved back into the right.

"All right, Thorny," I shot back. "No point in being an asshole about it."

She gave me a quick glare before putting her eyes back on the road. "Watch yourself, Zeezee."

"Zeezee!" yelled Pear from the back seat.

"If the Accountants take us out, they immediately rise in the scum pool of criminality that is Infernal City. That's true for *anyone* who drops us."

"No one is going to destroy the PPD," I said, my voice hard. "At least not while I'm breathing."

"Stopping your breathing…I think that's the plan."

"Rose, you insane excuse for a driver," Silk yelled. *"Are you trying to get us all killed?"*

"If you can't keep up, you should've stayed at the station,"

Rose said, slowing down and drifting into the left lane again. *"We have Accountants on our asses."*

"Oh, shit," Silk replied. *"Well, why are you slowing down, then? You plan on discussing debits and credits?"*

"Debits mostly," Rose said, drawing one of her hand cannons. *"It's time to remove them from this equation. Keep your pace up. Doe and Graffon, you're Alpha Two,"* Rose commanded. *"Silk and Butch, Alpha Three. Don't slow down. Pass me on the sides when I stop."*

"You're going to what?" I asked, aloud. "Did you say stop?"

"We can't have them following us to Bernie's," Rose replied, slowing down. "If I bring Accountants in my wake, he'll shoot me on principle alone for not shaking them."

The vehicles holding the rest of the team drifted out to either side.

"In position," Graffon said. *"Ready to move on your signal."*

"Same here," Butch confirmed. *"We'll overtake you and then swing around to flank them."*

"Good," Rose said, slowing down even more. *"When I stop, proceed as if abandoning us, then swing back."*

"Roger," Butch answered.

"Affirmative," Graffon replied. *"However, I must add that you will be alone with our pursuers for a total of thirty seconds. In that time, the danger—"*

"Shut it, Graf," Rose cut in. *"You can explain the statistical dangers after I deal with these idiots."*

Rose slammed on the brakes and brought us to a screeching stop. We slid for a few meters, leaving skid-marks on the road.

"Weee," bellowed Pear with glee as his face slammed into the headrest of my seat. "Do it again! Again!"

"Strange kid," Rose noted.

"If you only knew."

I pulled out Butterfly, not wanting to use Pinky and dragon rounds in the middle of the street.

Butterfly fired conventional rounds, which punched holes in anything I aimed at. Pinky used dragon rounds, which were as devastating as they sounded. They created a not-so-controlled explosion and left craters. I could only fire Pinky once every few minutes or I risked setting off a round in the weapon.

Dragon rounds were unstable and prone to detonation.

Pinky wasn't made for rapid fire.

"I'm ready," I said. "Let's arrest these—"

"What are you doing?" Rose asked, hooking a thumb behind us. "Who's going to watch the Shredder? Can you guarantee he'll remain contained in here?"

I glanced back at Pear, who was doing something between a semi-bounce and rocking. He waved at me when he saw me looking.

"ZeeZee," he said and went back to his rocking bouncing. "Can I smash my face again? That was fun!" Then, he sniffed the air. "Are bad men coming?"

"On second thought, you're right," I said. "I'll stay with Pear. You apprehend the Accountants. *Apprehend*, Rose... not disintegrate or perforate."

"And where am I going to put them, exactly, Zeezee?"

"Zeezee!"

"It's not like we have a prison van with us."

"My point is that you don't have to kill them," I said with a touch of angst.

"Unlikely," Rose scoffed, "but I'll do my best."

The two black vans pulled up next to us, one in front and one behind, cutting off any escape.

I almost felt sorry for them as Rose stepped out.

CHAPTER 16

*T*hey didn't do the right thing.

A pair of Accountants slid open the side door, jumped out of the rear van in wrinkled suits, and opened fire.

Rose pulled out her other gun and blasted the tires of the van, before having the Last Word, and closing the accounts on the two gunmen. Inside the van, a couple more tie-wearers opened fire as Rose ducked behind our vehicle. The van in front opened the side door, and I stared into the barrels of an XM556 Microgun. It was a handheld Gatling beast, designed to fire anywhere from two thousand to four thousand rounds per minute.

Our vehicle was covered in armor plating, but I had a feeling the rounds in the Microgun were armor piercing. I saw the barrel begin to rotate, grabbed Pear and rolled out of the vehicle, keeping the door open and using it as a shield as we made our way to the rear.

The high-pitched whine started as a hail of rounds cut into and through our vehicle. This was cut short by a sudden crash. I peeked around our car and saw Silk and Butch make their way to the van's driver. The guy looked unconscious. The Accountant who had opened fired was having a final conversation with Doe, who had lifted his veil and was currently sending the gunman into the depths of despair and darkness. Meanwhile, Graffon had cuffed and restrained the other Accountant in the rear and began explaining his rights as a suspect of attempted murder of a PPD officer.

Judging from the look on his face, I wouldn't be surprised if he begged someone to attempt to murder him. Demons and voids were, by far, some of the most psychologically fearsome beings in the Badlands. Hellions would rip your face off and a dragon might eat you, but demons and voids would make you end yourself and thank them for the privilege.

And with Graffon being a mix of both, well...yeah.

"Graffon," I said, loudly, "I'd like to ask him some questions. Try not to destroy his capacity for thought...or speech."

"Of course not, Chief," Graffon answered. "But he did fire on a PPD officer, which is a crime punishable by apprehension, incarceration, and extreme conversation."

"Just don't melt his brain," I said.

I moved to the other side, where Rose had redecorated the exterior of the rear van with the Accountant's head. I examined the dents in the van and assumed the Accountant Rose was holding was dead. The groan escaping his lips proved otherwise.

"I thought he was done...judging from the body work. How is he still alive?"

"This one is a hellion," Rose replied, shaking his limp body. "He can take a bit of punishment. He's still alive... for now."

"I need to ask him some questions," I said. "Do you think we can—?"

"No time," Rose said, lifting up the hellion and throwing him into Butch's vehicle."This is just a scouting party. More Accountants are on their way. We need to be gone by the time they get here."

"Our vehicle is done," I pointed out, looking at the smoking husk that used to be a method of transport. "I'll get a ride with Alpha Two. You jump in with Alpha Three."

Rose reached into the van and grabbed the Microgun.

"Never know when something like this might come in handy," she said, tapping the side of the weapon. *"Doe, get the gun from the van and bring ammo...all of it."* She closed the connector and said, "Here, Butch."

Butch placed the Microgun in the back with several cases of ammunition and shoved the Accountant out of the vehicle.

"What are you doing?" I asked. "We need to speak to him."

"Not much room, Chief," Butch answered. "What do you need more right now? The Accountant or guns and ammo?"

"Do you think we're going to run out of criminals after us?" Rose asked. "We need to get out of here."

They were right. I knew there would be no shortage of people coming after us. We did however, have a shortage of weapons and ammunition.

"Fine," I said with a groan. "We'll grab another one later on."

"That's the spirit," Rose said, jumping in the driver's seat and turning the engine on.

"Make sure the next one is grabbed by Butch," I said, glancing back at Graffon and Doe. "That way I can actually interrogate them."

Rose stared at us.

"Let's go!" she yelled. "There are more of these idiots on the way with more guns that fire an obscene number of rounds per minute."

The Accountants interrogated by Doe and Graffon were lying on the floor, drooling, twitching, and groaning. Asking them questions would be pointless.

"We need to go," I sighed.

"$\mathcal{I}$ thought I told you I needed to ask them some questions," I said, looking at the pair as I approached the vehicle. I climbed behind the wheel a few moments later. "How is that supposed to happen now?"

"Oh, look it's your little monst—brother," Doe said, getting in the backseat and sitting next to Pear. "Does it...*he* bite?"

"Only if you antagonize him," I said, glancing at Pear. "These are good people, Pear. Do *not* bite them, okay?"

"Maybe," Pear purred.

"That's reassuring," Doe said. "Does he usually listen to you?"

"Not really."

Doe nodded. "Can I shoot him?"

"You could try," I answered. "Probably lose your hand before you fired a round, though. Note that he doesn't like sudden movements."

"I'll keep that in mind, thanks," Doe said, keeping his hand away from his weapon.

"Now, quit deflecting," I said, irritated. "What happened back there? I specifically said I wanted to speak to those Accountants."

"I think we got a little carried away," Doe answered, adjusting his veil. "But not to worry, we're pretty certain they had no useful information."

"What do you mean *we?*" Graffon asked. "You were the one that unleashed the despairing darkness. Talk about getting carried away."

"You call that getting a *little* carried away?" I asked, looking at the Accountants, who were still twitching on the ground. "What's going to happen to them?"

"They'll be fine," Graffon said with a hand wave. "A few years of intense shock therapy should revert them to almost normal. Although, that one"—she pointed at the one Doe had 'interrogated'—"may need a brain removal."

"Brain removal? Is that even possible?"

"Perfectly safe on goblins," Graffon answered, getting in the passenger side next to me. "Statistics show most goblins only use one percent of their brains anyway. I doubt he'll even miss it."

Rose started her vehicle.

"Where are we going, Rose?" I asked over the comms. *"And can we get there before more of these Accountants show up with those Gatling guns?"*

"We need to pick up Bernie and then head to The Morgue," Rose replied, racing on ahead. *"Let's see if you can keep it up, Chief."*

"This isn't a race, Lieutenant," I stated, flooring the accelerator. *"I'd like to get there in one piece."*

Graffon sniffed. "*With the Lieutenant, it's always a race. We just never know where the finish line is.*"

"*More like a demolition race,*" Silk added. "*Did you know they had to make her car to special modifications? Nimble nearly lost his shit designing the upgrades to her car.*"

"*Shut it, both of you,*" Rose answered. "*The upgrades were necessary.*"

"*Took him an extra six weeks before he got the designs approved,*" Silk said. "*They thought he was designing some new kind of urban tank disguised as a PPD vehicle.*"

"*The budget for the Lieutenant's car did exceed the project costs... for the entire fleet,*" Graffon added. "*That year was very difficult financially for the PPD.*"

"*Her one car cost more than the entire fleet?*" I asked incredulously. "*How is that even possible?*"

"*Nimble was thrilled,*" Rose defended. "*Said so himself.*"

"*Right, like Nimble is going to tell you what a pain in the ass you are,*" Silk scoffed. "*He's a slug, you're a hellion...*" Silk paused. "*Hmmm, I wonder who loses in that equation?*"

"*I'd never attack Nimble,*" Rose said. "*He just irks me at times.*"

"*So the times you've threatened to slice him in two,*" Silk said, "*drawn your gun in the lab, caused Tam and Yarrl to physically defend him, were expressions of you being irked?*"

"*Yes, but if we continue this conversation, I'm going to get pissed,*" Rose said with a growl. "*And I'm going to squash a certain dark fae pain in my ass.*"

"*Don't forget the time she threatened to use her devastator on Nimble to see if he could clone himself,*" Graffon said with a smile. "*Something about having two of him would increase the lab's productivity. If I recall correctly, slugs are not capable of regeneration. Bifurcating Nimble would not cause two slugs, rather it would most likely be the cause of his demise."*

"Enough," Rose said. *"My car needed special mods because I'm a special driver—end of story."*

"Special driver?" Silk said with a barely contained laugh. *"Our 'special' lieutenant totaled three vehicles in one week. I heard the Directors were going to cut the vehicle budget if you kept destroying the fleet."*

"They kept giving me inferior vehicles," Rose countered. *"What do you want me to do with the P.O.S. vehicles they were unloading on me. I actually did the PPD a favor—getting rid of those crap cars."*

There was a pause before the comms erupted with laughter.

Honestly, I was just happy that they were picking on someone other than me at this point. I'd been the butt of most jokes since joining the PPD. I was the new guy, so I got it. Plus, being the chief didn't help much either. People always picked on authority. We were the easy target.

"Keep it up," Rose said, angrily. *"I will shoot you all in places that hurt."*

The laughter increased.

"I'll take my chances with your shooting over your driving," Silk replied. *"Did you let the chief know about the injury reports from last year?"*

"Injury reports?" I asked, swerving around a truck as Rose cut through traffic with ease. *"What injury reports? I didn't see any injury reports."*

More laughter followed by a long 'ooooooh' from Butch.

"Maybe you should break it to him when he isn't driving,"

Silk answered. *"Liable to cause him to lose control when he finds out."*

"How bad is it?" I asked. *"Graffon?"*

"Bad enough to require a special authorization from the Directors and force her to take classes with Bernard, or be suspended from the PPD," Graffon answered. *"Her driving was much worse before her classes."*

"Worse?" I said. *"How is that possible?"*

"When you see the reports, you'll know how," Graffon replied. *"The DMV—Demonic Ministry of Vehicles—classified the lieutenant as a Grade A liability."*

"Grade A liability?" I asked. *"That sounds like a good thing."*

"It's not," Doe stated. *"Not really."*

"It truly is quite impressive," Graffon said. *"Grade A liability is a classification reserved for acts of mass destruction, cataclysms, and the like. I don't believe that classification has been given to any one individual before."*

"Until the lieutenant," Silk chimed in, *"but that's a good description of her driving—an act of mass destruction."*

"Leave her alone, Silk," Butch said. *"Can't you see talking about her horrible driving bothers her?"*

"What bothers me," Rose started, *"is knowing that I'm going to have to waste rounds on your worthless asses if you keep this conversation going."*

"Hey, seriously," Silk asked, *"where are we going? It looks like we're heading into dragon territory."*

"Exactly," Rose replied. *"Bernie lives a few miles outside Infernal City, deep in dragon country."*

"But he's a hellion, right?" Butch said.

"That's exactly why he's in dragon country."

CHAPTER 18

"*S*ince when do dragons let a hellion live in their *territory?*" I asked, trying to stay close to Rose's vehicle. *"They hate each other."*

"Since they want to make life difficult for the hellions who would like to end him," Rose said. *"This has nothing to do with liking Bernie and everything to do with causing difficulty for hellions."*

"Does this have to do with his driving?" I asked, confused.

"Bernie has a few more skills besides driving," Rose answered. *"He worked for House Blaze as a cleaner, among other things."*

"He cleaned homes?"

"Sure...he cleaned homes...usually by exploding them with everyone inside," Silk said. *"Bernard Blaze is one scary hellion."*

"Aren't they all?"

"This is the hellion that scares all the other ones," Silk answered. *"No one messes with B.B."*

"He's an assassin?" I asked, not really surprised. This was Rose after all.

"More like Human Resources Fatal Conflict Resolution," Rose answered, jumping onto the sidewalk to avoid traffic, and a truck, before swerving back to the road. *"He was one of the best."*

I shook my head.

"Dragon territory," I said. *"Isn't this going to be dangerous for you?"*

"I'm going to go see Bernie, not have a meeting with dragons. I'll be granted safe passage."

Doe spoke up. *"We're going to get help from a criminal? I'm sure everyone here is aware already, but I find it concerning that the PPD is seeking the aid of a criminal."*

"He's a family friend," Rose noted.

"Who's a criminal," I replied, supporting Doe's point.

"You have a Valkyrie mother and a bragon 'I don't know what' for a brother."

"Neither of whom are crim..." I paused and thought back to the conference room where Pear shredded a Rider like tissue paper. Then I recalled Hilda's cooking, which definitely qualified as scandalous. *"Fine. Point made."*

The connector chatter died down for a minute, giving me time to look around. I hadn't been into the dragon zone since my early teens, before the incident. It was like I remembered, though. There was an uppityness about the place that filled the air.

"We're heading into the neutral zone to pick up weapons soon," Rose said seriously. *"You ever been out there, Chief?"*

"Not that I can recall, no."

"What do you think the land between the Badlands and Netherworld Proper is going to be filled with?"

"Sand and emptiness?" I answered. "Not much of anything?"

"Wrong," Rose said. "They know we're coming. It's going to be filled with criminals who want those weapons and who want us dead."

"So we're joining a criminal to face criminals?"

"You want to survive in the Badlands?" Rose asked. "Sometimes you have to be worse than the monsters you face... remember that."

She floored the accelerator and pulled away. I could tell she was clearly upset, well, more upset than usual.

While I agreed that sometimes being the law in the land of lawlessness was difficult, I didn't buy the sentiment that you had to become a criminal to stop a criminal. There were lines we couldn't cross. As chief, it was my job to make sure that, no matter how close we came to that line, we never stepped over it.

"Heads up," Silk announced, "dragon state line is only a few seconds away."

"Does this feel nostalgic, Chief?" Graffon asked, not using the connector. "Being near your kind must feel comforting."

"He was raised by valkyries," Doe reminded Graffon from the backseat. "His kind probably felt he was too proper to be among them. That's why he's chief."

It stung, but Doe was probably right. I had adhered to the valkyrie teachings of honor as far back as I could remember. It made my life among the valkyrie somewhat easier.

My entire life, I had heard that dragons were just creatures of destruction that killed without concern for the consequences. That wasn't me at all. If upholding honor, doing what's right, and avoiding what's wrong made me an outcast from my own kind, so be it.

I would do what I could to make sure the PPD was a place where the laws were upheld—that and the fact that I would be facing Hilda if I messed up, was not a pleasant option, and incredible motivation.

Entering dragon territory only reinforced my need to succeed as the chief of the Badlands Paranormal Police Department.

CHAPTER 19

*W*e passed the exorbitant estates of the dragons and followed a winding road deep into one of the properties.

"This is which estate?" I asked Graffon, who was looking out of the window. "Impressive."

"These are the estates of some of the older dragon families," Graffon answered. "Which makes sense. In order to protect a hellion with Bernard's reputation, House Blaze must have pulled some considerable strings."

"Like I said," Rose answered. *"He's a family friend."*

Apparently, I had set my connector to pick up normal discussions. This was an active protocol on the connector unit. You could either leave it shut off so that you could have private conversations, or you could allow people to listen in. It wouldn't catch everything in the area, but it was decent at picking up anything within a few meters. Essentially, if you could hear the voice well enough, it was likely that the connector could effectively broadcast it just as well.

"*That and the fact that not even an army of hellions would dare storm his home,*" Doe added. "*much less in dragon territory.*"

"*What did he do?*" I asked, tying directly into the conversation. "*What was so bad that he can't even live with hellions?*"

"*Everyone pay attention,*" Rose said. "*This way you'll know who and what you're dealing with, and I won't have to repeat myself or feel sorry if you get killed by Bernie.*"

"*You can feel sorry?*" Silk asked. "*Learn something new everyday.*"

"*I'm surprised she can feel...period,*" Butch added. "*That's really amazing for a hellion.*"

Both of them were living dangerously, considering they were in the same vehicle with Rose.

"*Both of you are going to feel my guns,*" Rose shot back, "*as I pistol whip you across the face.*"

"*There goes that warm, feeling hellion we all know and tolerate,*" Silk replied.

"*Shut it, you little fairy,*" Rose said as Silk replied with some curses in a language I couldn't make out. Funny thing about curses, doesn't matter the language—you know a curse when you hear one. "*Everyone pay attention because I'm not repeating this.*"

"*Got it,*" I said. "*Was he exiled?*"

"*Not exactly,*" Rose answered. "*He almost wiped out a House...alone.*"

"*Excuse me?*" I replied, frowning.

Alone?

I highly doubted that.

One of the things Hilda made me do was learn a fair

amount about the various laws in the land. Hellions, the nine levels, and, yes, even dragons.

For a hellion House to be taken out would require some serious effort and coordination. It typically involved multiple Houses, acting in synchronicity, to even have a *chance* at wiping out another House. Even then, the stakes were incredibly high. If a single person survived from the House being attacked, and they managed to survive for a full year, that person could come back to not only claim their rightful place as the head of their own House, they could also lay claim to the head of the Houses that attacked them.

So, again, I highly doubted that any single person could wipe out a House...even 'almost.'

"What do you mean he almost wiped out a House?" I asked.

"On his last job, he was doing a run for House Rancor—"

"House Rancor was almost eliminated some time ago," Graffon said. *"Everyone thought it was internal hellion politics."*

"It wasn't," Rose said. *"Bernard discovered they were going to assassinate him after the job."*

"So he sought to take them out first?" I asked, confused. *"And the other Houses were okay with this?"*

"They didn't know," Rose replied. *"If they had, he would have been stopped instantly."*

"His own House would have had to agree with his decision, too," Graffon noted. *"I'm assuming that wasn't the case here?"*

"He told them nothing, either," Rose said. *"But Bernard still operated within hellion law and almost eliminated everyone in House Rancor,"* Rose said.

Graffon coughed lightly. *"I fail to see how he operated*

within hellion law. To do so, he would have had to been given the full endorsement of his own House, which you have already claimed he didn't even seek."

"*Graffon is correct,*" Rose confirmed, "*but only based on today's hellion law, which has been rewritten to avoid this ever happening again.*" She paused. "*The original law held a loophole that allowed anyone under direct threat from an enemy House to take matters into their own hands, doing what they could to eradicate the offending House should the individual member deem the cause worthy.*"

Graffon nodded as she studied the datapad. "*That change was entered into the books thirty-seven years ago, prior to my deeper study of hellion law. I stand happily corrected. Thank you, Rose.*"

"*Uh, yeah, sure,*" Rose replied. "*Anyway, he nearly wiped out House Rancor, but they caught on before the bombs he'd placed had fully detonated.*"

"*Bombs?*"

"*Yep. He loaded the House with them and sent out a general order to have everyone attend the great hall for a mandatory meeting.*" She chuckled. "*It was a brilliant plan, but one of the wires on the explosives connection shorted out and only half the place came down.*"

"*Not very thorough, then?*" I asked.

"*Shit happens,*" she defended her friend. "*Well, he got away, but when word got out about what he'd done, all the Houses felt he was too dangerous to live. They executed a general kill order on him, including his own House.*"

"*A general kill order?*" Graffon asked. "*That's unprecedented. For all the Houses to come to an agreement like that meant Bernard was a real and present threat.*"

"*He was,*" Rose answered, "*and probably still is. Do not piss him off.*"

We continued down the winding road for some time until we came to a smaller version of the larger estate homes.

Outside the home stood a hellion dressed in combat leathers, holding a small bag. A larger bag rested by his feet. He was average height and above-average menace.

His gray hair was cut short to the scalp, and I could see he kept himself in fighting shape. A hellion who could almost take down an entire House alone would be a ferocious combination of intelligence, cunning, and lethality.

Rose was right, we didn't want to piss him off.

"Do all hellions wear combat leathers?" I asked as we approached.

"Yes, and no," Graffon answered. "A hellion's central philosophy is: a fight may occur at any moment, better to be armed and not need it, than need it and not have it. But some dignitaries or priests will just carry a stiletto or something."

"So, the weapons are a default grab for them, despite the fact that they're the ones that usually start most of the fights?"

"That fact doesn't seem to factor into their general philosophy," Graffon replied, "but it must influence their wardrobe choices."

"Right," I said, looking at Bernard. I then focused back on the connector. "*He can ride shotgun with you, Lieutenant.*"

"*Good idea, since he really can't stand dragons,*" Rose answered, "*or pretty much anyone who isn't a hellion. And do note that some hellions refuse to carry around weapons, considering themselves weaponly enough."*

"Weaponly?" I asked, and then quickly added, *"Never mind. So, you just implied that Bernard doesn't know I'm a dragon. Is this going to be a problem?"*

"Not for him," Rose said. *"Just stay away until I explain things."*

"This is going to go over well then."

"It's possible he's softened his stance on dragons, since they did help him," Rose offered. *"He may not like you, but I'm pretty sure he can tolerate you."*

"Lovely," I said with a groan. *"Just what we need on this trip: an angry, super assassin hellion."*

"My thoughts exactly," Rose said. *"He'll fit right in."*

CHAPTER 20

*B*ernard approached the vehicles as we pulled to a stop in front of his home.

"Thorny!" he said as Rose grimaced. "You brought friends. Never thought I'd see the day you'd actually have friends."

"They aren't my friends," Rose answered with a growl. "We're co-workers."

"You aren't trying to shoot them," Bernard said. "I'm saying they're friends. Is that a dragon?"

He pointed at me.

"Bernard..." Rose started. "I can explain."

"No need," he said walking over to where I stood. "I heard the new chief was a dragon, just didn't think it was true. You survived the funeral party. Impressive."

"I had help," I admitted. "Lieutenant Blaze was instrumental in keeping me alive."

"She must be going soft then," Bernard answered. Everyone held their breath for a few seconds, before he cracked a smile, and an outstretched hand.

"Bernard Blaze, *almost* destroyer of House Rancor and mentor to the insanity you call a second-in-command."

I shook his hand and felt the crushing strength in his grip. This was not a hellion to piss off. He looked around at our group and nodded.

"Ezekias Phoenix," I said. "Chief of the Badlands Paranormal Police Department."

"Which is currently in deep shit from what I hear. Holy tittyballs, is that a bragon?" he asked, looking at Pear. "I haven't seen one of them in ages. Ferocious fuckers, but not too sharp."

I nodded. "That pretty much sums him up," I said. "That's my little brother, Pear."

"Shit, you must be expecting serious trouble if you brought one of them."

"I'm kind of babysitting," I said, under my breath. "He's not really part of the team."

Bernard stepped close to Pear, who smelled the air around him.

"You don't really want to get too close to him because —" I started.

Bernard made some guttural noises followed by growls, hisses, and clicks. Pear's eyes widened, and he responded with the same kind of sounds.

"He really likes you," Bernard said, after Pear finished. "Doesn't think you're too bright, but most dragons aren't anyway. No offense."

"Some taken. You were just speaking a language I've never heard before."

"What, Bragon?" he replied, looking at me dubiously.

"He's your brother and you don't know how to speak in his native tongue?"

"I didn't know he had a native tongue."

"They do," Bernard stated with a nod toward Pear. "It's quite evolved as languages go, too, but since they're so rare, no one speaks it anymore. Bedsides, who's going to risk losing limbs by getting close enough to learn it?"

"Good point."

"You should make an effort to learn it, if you survive this little trip," he said and then glanced at Rose. "The kid is your brother, for fucksake." After a disappointed shake of his head, he turned to face Rose. "Thorny, lets roll. We have people to shoot and weapons to pick up."

He grabbed his bags and put them in the rear of Rose's vehicle.

"You want me to drive?" Rose said with an evil smile. "We're headed to The Morgue."

"Sure," Bernard said. "I haven't had breakfast yet, and our destination seems about right if you're driving."

"Fuck you, Bernie."

We drove down the winding road and left dragon territory, right into a welcoming committee of six black vans. They were parked alongside the road and fell in behind us as we passed.

"Remember the Accountant scouting party?" Doe asked, looking out the rear window. "The ones we left slightly incapacitated?"

"You mean the ones who were drooling on the ground in a vegetative state?"

"They were still alive," Doe countered, "which in my opinion, is considerable restraint."

"Yes, I recall," I said. "Are these the rest of the group?"

"Not entirely," Doe answered. "This is about half. I'm guessing the other half will meet up with us in transit once they know where we're going."

"Who leads this group?" I asked. "Maybe we can speak some sense into them."

"Harry Richard Blahck," Graffon said. "He won't be in any of the vans. He prefers to give instructions from their HQ."

"Harry Richard?" I asked. "Not Slasher or The Creditor or something like that? Harry Richard seems kind of boring."

"These are accountants, not commandos, boring comes with the package," Doe answered. "They will, however, shoot you with extreme prejudice. Their mini-Gatling guns, as you may recall, are quite exciting, especially if you're on the receiving end."

"I've seen them, thanks," I said, keeping one eye on the rearview mirror. "I'll pass."

"*Get off the Strip,*" Rose ordered through the connector. "*We'll never lose them here without collateral damage.*"

"*You mean the unsuspecting people or the other vehi—?*"

"*I mean damage to our rides,*" Rose said. "*Now stay close.*"

She pulled off the Strip and made a hard right into the outskirts of the city.

CHAPTER 21

*W*e were in the middle of nowhere with open land to either side of us. The lights of Infernal City grew distant with each passing second as the vans fell into a semi-circular formation behind us.

I looked in the rear-view mirror and saw the vans had sliding doors on both sides.

"That can't be good," I said, stepping on the accelerator. *"Accountants closing in."*

"They're going to use their guns, fall back into their formation," Rose said.

"So they can shoot us from both sides?" I countered. *"That sounds like a genius plan."*

"Trust me, I know what I'm doing," Rose said, slowing down. *"If they kill you in a hail of bullets, you can scream at me afterwards. Worst case, at least we're headed to the right place. Francis will give you a proper dragon burial—whatever that is."*

"Your sense of humor is almost as good as your driving," I

shot back. *"If they kill us, you get to answer to Hilda... remember that."*

"Duly noted," Rose answered. *"Slow down for a few seconds, and we'll take it from there. I just need you to distract them. Go!"*

I slowed down our vehicle and noticed the vans all had their side doors open with Gatling guns pointed...at us.

"Rose...?"

"A little busy at the moment. Hang tight and keep pace with them."

I saw her vehicle dart across the formation and pull up on the outside of the semicircle. I was about to speed out of the semi-circle of death when I caught sight of the passenger door opening on Rose's vehicle.

Bernard jumped and landed in one of the vans. He attacked and stripped a Gatling gun from one of the Accountants.

"Chief," Rose asked, *"do you want to get shredded to little dragon bits?"*

"Not particularly, no."

"Then get your ass out of there now!"

"You told me to slow down!"

"For a few seconds," Rose snapped. *"Not to stay there and be target practice. Move!"*

I stepped on the accelerator as rounds punched into the side of our vehicle. One of the vans swerved off to the side and rolled, bursting into flames. They were still in pursuit, but their numbers had been cut to four.

In the rear-view mirror, I saw Bernard grab a driver and eject him out of a van. He then slammed the van he was driving into another of the Accountant's vehicles, before leaping out and landing on the ground in a roll.

The vans skidded to a stop.

Gatling guns were firing everywhere among the Accountants. Bernard grabbed a handful of small hockey puck-shaped items from a pocket, tossed them at the Accountants and ran. Rose drifted her vehicle next to the running Bernard, as she opened the passenger door. With a hard pull to the right, she angled her vehicle to allow Bernard to run into the passenger side. She then turned the wheel the other way and took off.

A series of explosions followed as we put distance between us and the wreckage of Accountants. One hellion had just taken out six Accountants' vans, almost single-handedly. I had only seen Rose in action before today, but Bernard showed me why hellions were feared in the Badlands and beyond.

"That was an impressive display of destruction," Graffon said, staring behind us. "It looks like they managed to destroy all of the Accountants' vans."

"I noticed that," I said, glancing in the rearview mirror. "I still would've liked to ask them how they got the information."

"I'd say it's a little late for that, Chief," Graffon said with a smile. "They are a mangled mess."

"A mangled mess," I mused. "That kind of describes my day right about now."

CHAPTER 22

*W*e circled back and headed into the Infernal City.

"Can we take a route that avoids the up-and-coming criminals looking to make a name for themselves?" I asked. "I'm getting a little tired of being shot at today."

"We can take the old way to get to The Morgue," Doe said from the back. "It would avoid most, but not all, of the groups after us."

"That would be fucking great," I said and then remembered Pear was in the vehicle with us. "Shit."

"Fuckinggreatshitfuckinggreatshitfuckinggreatshit!" Pear yelled as he bounced around the back seat. "ZeeZee, fuckinggreatshit!"

"Oh, that's special," Doe noted in a calm voice, looking at the bouncing Pear. "Can I shoot him now?"

"Absolutely not," I said. "Pear...Pear! Sit down! Stop jumping around back there."

"ZeeZee!" Pear screamed at eardrum piercing levels. "ZeeZee!"

"I have a question, ZeeZee," Doe said, rubbing the ear closest to Pear.

"ZeeZee!"

"What?" I asked.

"Do you think bringing a child on this trip was really a good idea? We're clearly going to be chased and shot at for the duration of this mission."

"He's not a child," I said. "Just looks like one."

"And acts like one, too," Doe said, keeping an eye on Pear. "Albeit, one that's suffered brain trauma. The question still stands. Is it safe to bring him?"

"I have no choice," I answered, pressing a finger against my temple, trying to block out Pear's annoying voice. "I have to watch him and that means he stays close."

"Maybe we can leave him at The Morgue?" Doe asked. "I'm sure Francis wouldn't mind a little bundle of nervous energy."

"Is there anything remotely dangerous in The Morgue?"

"The Morgue coolant system uses pentafluroethane—a flammable refrigerant," Graffon started. "In addition, Francis is in possession of several creatures that have proven notoriously difficult to kill."

"Meaning?" I questioned, following Rose down a backroad behind the Strip on the dragon side. "Where does he have these 'creatures' currently?"

"They are in stasis."

"You mean they're alive?"

"That is what *in stasis* means," Graffon clarified. "I did say they were notoriously difficult to kill."

"Yes, but I thought they were *all* dead. Not slightly dead, but mostly alive."

"Actually," Graffon replied, "they are mostly dead, but slightly alive."

It really didn't matter what I said or did, there'd be an argument. If I had suggested that the creatures were mostly dead, but slightly alive, they'd have argued that they were slightly dead, but mostly alive.

There just wasn't a winning scenario with these two.

"Are you saying it's too dangerous to leave Pear there?"

"I'm assuming he's a hybrid of sorts," Graffon answered. "Most likely a dragon with something else. If he is dragon, and releases an uncontrolled flame inside The Morgue, it could set off the largest chain reaction explosion in the history of the Badlands."

"That bad?"

"The area known as The Morgue would have to be changed to The Wasteland, if that's any indication. In addition...some of those hard to kill creatures—"

"They'd make it through the blast wouldn't they?" I interrupted.

"They would survive the blast and be free to roam Infernal City."

"We're not leaving Pear with Francis." I then looked in the rearview mirror and quickly added, "Or Fitz," in case Doe had any other great ideas.

"Oh," Doe said. "In that case, nevermind."

"Really?" I replied, finding that strange. "You *were* going to suggest Fitz, weren't you?"

"Possibly," Doe replied. "He's a good assistant, solid, and has his head on straight...most days."

Well, that was out. First off, I had no desire to see a massive crater end up in the middle of the Badlands because I wasn't a fan of babysitting my brother. Hilda would rip my ass apart for that. Of course, so would the rest of the Badlands populace, and rightly so.

"You'll have to get used to Pear," I said, adding in a mischievous smile. "You never know, he may grow on you."

"Graffon," Doe asked, ignoring my last comment, "do you know if voids can melt their own brains?"

"I have tried it," Graffon answered with a shake of her head.

"Wait, what?" I asked, glancing sideways at her. "You did what?"

Then something caught my eye straight ahead.

In the distance was a squat, brown, windowless building that formed part of the exterior of The Morgue.

"Unfortunately, I was unsuccessful," Graffon answered with a soft sigh. "It would seem voids are immune to their own abilities."

"Fuck me," Doe muttered. "I won't make the whole trip with your little creature...er...er...brother, Chief. You should just shoot me—"

"FuckmeFuckmefuckmeeeeeee!" Pear yelled.

"If you could refrain from certain words he seems to pick up on," I winced, "you wouldn't have to deal with those outbursts."

"Or you could shoot me and then I won't have to hear them at all."

"He does seem to have a preference for certain words,"

Graffon observed. "Mostly the curses. This may have to do with a type of selective hearing and association."

The only thing that I could think of that was worse than Pear belting out colorful expletives, was Graffon giving us a dissertation regarding word choices that my little brother was selecting to belt out.

"Graffon," I interrupted, "do us all a favor."

"Yes, Chief?" Graffon said, looking back at Pear.

"Don't try to analyze him," I said. "His brain defies all explanation."

"I was just—" Graffon started.

"Trust me," I said. "It's too dangerous, even for a demonoid."

"We're here!" I heard Silk yell over the connector.

We had arrived at The Morgue.

$\mathcal{T}$he Morgue hadn't changed much since my last visit.

It was the simplest building you could imagine. There were no distinguishing features, colorful markings, or even a bit of shrubbery edging...which I think was the point. The one thing it *did* have was a ton of security. There were so many guards around the property, that it seemed more like a fort than a place to store dead bodies.

After my last visit, and meeting Francis, I realized the security wasn't to keep people out. The Morgue, along with the armed personnel policing it, existed to keep things *in* the facility.

Rose's words came back to me.

"Creatures get out of The Morgue enough times to make it dangerous," she'd said. "Things that are supposed to be dead don't stay dead, or they start out dead and then get less dead. Complete pain in the ass."

We were at ground level, which was just the main hall. Several levels below us sat the actual Morgue, but you had to go up through the main lobby to get there. Squat refrigeration units covered the area to either side of the entrance for what seemed like a mile or more. They maintained the environment of The Morgue, and, no, they could not be considered decoration. In fact, they looked like rusted old blocks of metal.

We got to the entrance and approached the heavily armed guards waiting for us. After a quick reveal of our ID badges, the doors swung open and we headed up the stairs.

Rose nodded at one of the guards at the next entrance. He returned a bro-nod, doing a quick scan of the rest of us. I couldn't see their faces due to the helmets that connected to their body armor. But, one by one, they let us through, checking our PPD badges in the process. Something about Pear made them step back. He seemed to have that effect on people. Probably the creepy smile filled with sharp fangs. Everything was smooth sailing.

Until they got to Bernard. They stopped him.

"ID please," the guard said, pointing at Bernard. "Sir?"

Rose stopped just after checkpoint and pointed at the guard with the name tag that read 'Allen.'

"You didn't brief the greenhorn?" she asked.

"Certainly did," Allen answered. "Smith here likes his rules."

"Smythe," the first guard said. "Not Smith."

"You must be new," Rose said, looking at the guard's name. "Smith with a Y?"

"Smythe, ma'am," the guard answered, pronouncing it with the long 'i' sound. Allen shook his head. "Not Smith, the Y is a long 'i' sound."

Rose nodded knowingly.

"Smythe?" Rose asked. "With a long 'i'?"

Everyone else stepped away from the guard.

"Twenty says she shoots him," Silk said under his breath.

Before the guard could respond, Rose drew both of her handcannons. One rested under the guard's chin and the other in his crotch.

"Let me explain how this is going to work...Smith with a long 'i'," Rose said with a smile that only inspired fear. "Paying attention? Nod slowly if you understand."

Smythe nodded slowly.

"Good," she said. "You see that old, broken down hellion over there?"

She pointed at Bernard with her chin, and Smythe nodded.

"Hey?" Bernard said. "I'm not broken down."

"He's with us," Rose said, ignoring Bernard. "That means he's coming inside...without ID. Are we clear?"

Smythe nodded again.

"Next time," Rose said, looking at Allen, "brief the rookies the right way or I shoot the seniors...starting with you." She poked the gun into Smythe's crotch, causing him to double over. "You think we have time for these games?"

"Yes, ma'am," Allen said, flustered. "I mean no ma'am. I'll make sure it doesn't happen again."

"See that it doesn't," Rose stated and walked inside. She holstered her guns just as fast as she'd drawn them. "Let's go."

Bernard shook his head at the rest of the team, and then followed Rose in. I hung back with him.

"Was she always like this?" I asked.

"You mean her sweet, pleasing disposition?" Bernard answered with a smile. "You should've seen her when I first started training her"—Bernard placed a hand on Smythe's shoulder—"ten years ago she would've shot you in the berries instead of just giving them a bit of a tap. Be happy she's mellowed with age."

"Mellowed?" I said to myself as we stepped inside The Morgue.

CHAPTER 24

"Welcome…welcome," Francis said, stopping in his tracks when he saw Pear. "Is that a—?"

"No," I said. "I mean yes, it's a bragon and no, you can not experiment or examine him."

I looked at the smallish figure dressed in a white lab coat. His hair was a disheveled orange explosion covering piercing green eyes, which stared at me from behind a pair of thick-rimmed glasses. A pocket protector peeked out from the lab coat, holding an assortment of pens and instruments.

"A pity..really," Francis replied. "Bragons are so rare. To have a live one to work on…I mean examine…" He cleared his throat. "Are you sure?"

"If you knew who his mother was, you wouldn't be asking that question."

"Really? Is his mother a bragon, too?"

"Not quite," I said. "Do you know who Hilda is?"

"The leader of the Dragon's Teeth valkyries?" Francis

asked. "Yes, she sends plenty of business our way." His eyes suddenly shot open. "Wait, are you saying that—"

"I'm saying that," I stated with a nod. "Still want to examine the bragon?"

"On second thought," Francis answered, shaking his head. "There's no need. Angering her would be unwise."

"No argument there, pal," I sighed. "Take it from someone who grew up with her."

Francis gave me an appraising look. "She raised you? Curious."

Behind him, lumbered the mismatched figure of Fitz.

"Fitz, baby," Silk said, "how are you holding up?"

Fitz nodded and groaned.

"Me too, Fitzy," Silk answered. "Me too."

Fitz was the essence of a made man...literally.

He stood as tall as a troll, had the head of a goblin, and the arms of a valkyrie. I didn't know much about his brain, or if he even had one. The last time I saw him, he had come apart at the seams due to the pressure...the pressure of an exploding hellion.

"Good to see you again, Fitz," I said. "In one piece, at least."

More groans.

"Francis," I said, turning back toward the examiner, "I hear you have some vehicles for us?"

"Ah, yes," Francis said, giving us a quick nod and hurrying off. "They're in the garage. This way."

Francis was moving like a speedy little goblin. He *wasn't* a goblin, or at least he didn't look like one. The fact was that nobody really knew precisely what he was, and it wasn't exactly polite to ask.

He was somewhat more chilled the first time I'd met him.

"Is it me, or does Francis seem extra jumpy today?" I asked Rose as we followed him.

"You work with the dead and semi-dead long enough," Rose answered, looking around, "it takes a toll. He was unstable even before he worked here, of course. I'm guessing this place is just making it worse."

I glanced around and noticed more guards on the floor than last time.

A lot more.

Francisly, if there had been this many guards the last time we were here, things would have gone a lot more smoothly.

There were literally rows of them.

"Is Francis expecting an invasion or something?" I asked. "Why the extra security?"

Rose glanced around.

"I noticed that too," she said under her breath. Then looked ahead. "Francis? You expecting an attack? What's with the extra manpower?'

That was Rose. The definition of subtle.

"After your last visit, I decided I didn't have enough security personnel on the premises," Francis answered. "It appears The Morgue's external threats are a greater priority than any of my current residents."

The answer made sense, considering what had happened last time, but his body language was off.

Unfortunately, I couldn't have this conversation privately with Rose. The Morgue was shielded inside and out, jamming all signals, making the connectors impossible to use, even at close range.

"Lieutenant," I said, giving her a look, "once we get the vehicles, let's contact the station. I'd like a situation update."

Rose glanced at me, obviously catching my expression.

"Understood," she answered. Then added, "I really hope these Deadhaul things are durable, or this is going to be a short roadtrip."

$\mathcal{W}$e followed Francis down a ramp to the lower level.

Pear raced to the bottom and back to the top several times before we reached the lower level. How someone his age had that much energy was a testament to the strange mixture of werebear and dragon DNA. There were a few benefits, and quite a few disadvantages.

At the foot of the ramp, the enormity of The Morgue hit me.

The area we stood in was a garage. Several trucks of varying sizes sat in parking bays. The ceilings were easily thirty feet tall, which explained why it had taken so long to traverse the stairs. And the signage pointing this way had said 'Small Garage.' This 'small' section dwarfed our entire station several times over. I couldn't even imagine what the 'Large Garage' looked like.

"This place is huge," I said in awe. "How do you manage such a large facility?"

"I have plenty of help," Francis answered. "Some I hire,

and some I make. Over there"—he pointed to a group of trucks—"Deadhaul Division one."

"Division one?"

"This facility, Chief," Francis explained, extending his arms to his sides, "meaning the entirety of the building, of course, is the largest operating business in all of the Badlands for a reason."

"Death?"

"Yes!" Francis said, pointing at me and walking over to the Deadhaul Division. "The Badlands greatest feature, what drives it, what makes it work is...death."

"And that's where you come in," I said, looking at the Deadhauls. "You handle the death."

"It's a gruesome business," Francis replied, not looking bothered in the least, "but someone must do it. We provide a necessary service to Infernal City."

I gave him a nod and then examined the Deadhauls.

They were squat, armored, boxlike trucks with large cargo areas, I assumed to carry corpses. If The Morgue ever became militarized though, it could take over the Badlands on its own. Outfit a few of those Accountants' Gatling guns on these babies and you'd have a formidable armada.

"You need armored vehicles to transport bodies?" I asked, looking at the run-flat tires on each of the Deadhauls. "Isn't this a bit of overkill?"

"Some of the bodies we transport don't remain dead," Francis answered, stepping over to a small box that was anchored to the wall. "In those cases, it's best to have a way to keep the recently deceased contained."

He pressed a thumb to the small box and it clicked

open. Then he turned and glanced at the group before removing three small keycards. They were numbered from one to three. He handed me card one and Rose card two.

"That card goes to Bernard," I said, pointing at him when Francis looked confused about who to hand the last card to. "He's our lead driver."

Francis handed Bernard the last card.

"Please don't lose those," Francis stated. "The Deadhauls won't start without them."

"Good to know," Rose noted, putting her card in a pocket.

I tucked mine away in my chest pocket. If anyone wanted to get it from me, they'd have to lift it off my corpse. I wasn't exactly a fan of that idea, but seeing as I'd be hightailing it to the Vortex should I be killed, I wouldn't likely care who'd taken the trucks at that point.

"What are the specs on these, Francis?" asked Rose as she placed a hand on one of the massive tires.

"Right," Francis said with a nod. "The chassis of each of the trucks is made of polycarbon armor."

Graffon nodded. "Polycarbon armor can stop rockets and RPGs."

"And keep trolls inside," Francis added. "Especially when they get angry."

"The tires are run-flats?" I asked.

"Deadhauls are equipped with titanium run-flats," Francis answered. "Nothing in the Badlands can destroy one of these tires."

"What about fuel?" Doe asked. "How often will we need to refuel?"

"Deadhauls are tribrids," Francis replied. "You have solar cells fused to the armor, which power a solid-state battery that will give you nearly five hundred kilometers on one charge. They can keep a minimal charge, to ensure the battery is never fully drained."

"On one charge?" Rose asked with an eyebrow up. "That's impressive."

"Indeed," Francis agreed. "However, damage to the solar cells will impact the charging capabilities."

"Something to keep in mind," I said. "How long is a full charge, and what other fuels do these things run on?"

"The downside is that a full charge takes twelve to fifteen hours. I'd only use it in case of emergencies."

"No, shit," Silk said. "Only way we've stopped for that long is because we're dead."

"If that happens to occur," Francis said with a nod, "The Morgue will be happy to pick up your remains...free of charge. Provided there's anything left to pick up."

"Free of charge?" Silk shot back. "Feeling much better now, thanks."

"You're welcome," Francis answered. "We pride ourselves on our service."

"We have solar, electric, and what else?" I asked. "We can't power the solar cells if it becomes too overcast."

"True," agreed Francis. "Deadhauls are equipped to use conventional fuel with an auxiliary fuel tank system. This will be your primary source of fuel."

"How much can each tank hold?" I asked.

"Your primary tank will hold sixty gallons, and your auxiliary tank will hold an additional twenty gallons."

"How far on a full tank?" I asked.

"About ten kilometers per gallon," Francis answered. "Not the highest fuel efficiency."

"We're going to need to refuel at least twice on the way there and twice on the way back," I breathed. "Do we have locations of fuel stations?"

"Locations have been input into the onboard data system of each Deadhaul," Francis answered. "Easy to use and similar to your datapads. You won't need to refuel if you manage the energy systems judiciously, though."

"All these bells and whistles are as nifty as two hookers at half-price," Bernard chimed in, "but I just need to know one thing."

"And that is?" Francis asked, furrowing his brow. "I *do* believe I've covered everything."

"Nah, you missed the most important part," Bernard countered. "How fast can these fuckers go?"

CHAPTER 26

"Top speed is dependent on the laden weight, energy capacity, and terrain," Francis answered. "I'm afraid I can't give you an accurate velocity without knowing those variables."

"I have a related question," I said. "Can we use all the sources of fuel at once?"

Francis rubbed his chin in thought for a second. "I suppose its theoretically possible," he said. "We've never tried it, but I don't think the Deadhaul's engine or transmission can take that much force for a prolonged period of time."

"Good to know," I said. I reached into my pocket and pulled the keycard back out, handing it to Graffon. "Change of plans. You're driving one of these beasts."

Graffon looked down at the keycard and then back at me. I nodded.

"Are you certain about this, Chief?" Graffon asked. "I'm not as reckless as the Lieutenant."

"Precisely," I said. "Means at least one shipment will make it back." I then turned to look at the team. "Designations are as follows: Alpha One will be Rose, me, and"—I pointed at my brother—"him. We'll be running rear and defense. Alpha Two is Bernard, Silk and Butch. You'll be running point. Alpha Three will be Doe and Graffon. Any questions?"

Graffon raised her hand slowly.

"You don't have to raise your hand, Graffon," Rose snapped "What is it?"

"Well, if I'm going to be driving," Graffon started, "I can't use my regular name. It wouldn't be proper."

I frowned at her.

That seemed like an odd thing to say, but when dealing with Graffon you never quite knew what was going through her head. Typically, she followed up questions with overtly detailed responses that made you squint and wince a lot, so I wanted to be a little careful here.

"You want to change your name?" I asked, slowly.

"Not *change* my name," Graffon answered and took a short breath. "According to the BTU—the Badlands Trucking Union—Local One rule book, chapter two, subchapter 4.7, paragraph 6, every driver operating a vehicle of the truck class must use an official designator in place of their given name."

"You want a...handle?" I asked.

"It's a union rule, sir."

"But you're not in the union, Graffon."

"At this exact moment," she replied, looking a bit drawn, "you are absolutely correct. However, if you jump to Appendix C of the BTU rules, and flip three pages to

Amendment 18, you'll find that any person, male, female, or other, and regardless of race, is considered to be under the temporary employ of the union from the moment they sit in the driver's seat of the truck until the moment they evacuate said seat."

We all blinked at her.

"It should also be noted that this amendment extends to persons who are dead or alive."

We blinked faster, and there may have been a few of us rubbing our temples.

"So..." I started and stopped, grimacing at her for a few seconds. "One of these days, you'll have to tell me how you know all of this."

"Oh, well, it's quite a case of—"

"*One* of these days, Graffon," I interrupted with my hand held up. "*Not* today."

"Sorry, Chief."

I took in a deep breath and calmed myself. Having a Graffon-induced migraine, or, as the rest of the team had come to call it, a Migraffon, was not conducive to the mission on which we were about to embark upon.

"Do you know what you'd like your handle to be?" I asked, feeling incredibly uncomfortable at having to pose the question.

"How about Loquacious Lunatic?" Rose volunteered.

"I've given this some thought," Graffon replied, clearly ignoring Rose's suggestion.

"You have?" I asked. "When did you have time to—never mind." I shook away the question. "Sorry. What handle did you have in mind?"

"I was thinking of Smart Succubus," she said, smartly.

More blinks.

"I am half demon and quite intelligent," Graffon added, "so it kind of works. What do you think?"

"Well," I said, feeling like we were walking into territory that would eventually land us all in the Human Resources department, "first of all, succubi aren't demons."

"That's correct, Chief," Graffon said. "Well done."

"Uh…thanks?" I said, feeling lost. "Wait…if you know that a succubus is not a demon, why did you feel the need to point out that you're half demon?"

"To demonstrate that I was being clever, Chief," she answered.

I went to ask another question, but decided to just let it go.

"So," I stated, just as Pear had run back to the group from the other side of the garage, "Smart Succubus?"

"Suckyourbuttsuckyourbuttsuckyourbutt!" Pear yelled. "ZeeZee! Suck…your…butt!"

I grabbed him by the collar and ushered him to the Deadhaul, closed the door, and turned slowly back to face my team.

Everyone remained silent for a few seconds before erupting in laughter.

"Smart Suckyourbutt!" Silk yelled and then cackled. "Starting to really like that kid." His face went suddenly still and he snapped his fingers. "How about smart suck my—"

"I think…Succubus is appropriate," Bernard interrupted, ending the laughter. He picked up his bag and headed to his

Deadhaul. "Honestly, I couldn't give two nipples what the hell you all call yourselves. All I care about is that you keep the formation tight, and you get the job done."

"You do?" Rose asked.

"For the record," Bernard added, raising his voice, "if anyone calls me anything other than Bernard, I'll end you and dump your body on the side of the road."

"Roger that, B.B.," Rose said.

Bernard returned a one finger salute before getting into his Deadhaul.

"Graffon, we all know you're smart," I said. "If you're going to use a handle how about something with a little punch. You are half void after all. Why not something like Dark Smarty?"

"That's lame, Chief," Silk said.

"Smarty Dark?"

"Even worse," stated Doe.

"Fine," I said, throwing my hands up. "What about Dark Succubus, then?"

The moment the words exited my lips, I knew I shouldn't have said them.

"Dark Succubus?" Graffon said, repeating it a few times to herself, and glaring at Silk. "I like that. Thank you, Chief."

I sighed as my shoulders drooped. "Swell."

"My name is going to be Pain Goddess," Rose announced with an evil smile. "On account of how much pain I'm going to give each of you if you don't get in your trucks...now."

"How about we just call you Angry Hemorrhoid?" Silk

asked, dodging a swipe from Rose. "You're still a pain... just a pain in the ass."

Everyone headed to their Deadhauls. Francis stepped over to my side of the vehicle, and I lowered the plexan window.

"Nimble facilitated a sizable deposit for each of these vehicles," Francis noted. "The odds of your return are slim to none, after all."

"He told me," I said. "Your point?"

"Each of the Deadhauls features a self-destruct switch located"—he pointed inside the vehicle—"underneath there, right next to the rockets."

"Rockets?" I asked. "Why would a Deadhaul need rockets?"

"On occasion, velocity is required," Francis replied. "In those situations, you'll find a rocket enhanced engine —useful."

"I can't believe this thing has rockets," I said under my breath. "What else does it do?"

"If you find yourself in dire straits, sacrifice one or all of the Deadhauls, but do try to make it back alive."

"Francis," Rose started, her voice hard, "I didn't know you cared."

"I don't," Francis replied with the same tone, "but the uptick in business that will be the result of your deaths will be more than The Morgue can handle presently. The Badlands without the PPD leadership is bad for business."

"I'm touched, really," I said, shaking my head. "I'll keep that in mind if we find ourselves in 'dire straits' during this trip. Thanks again for the Deadhauls."

"It was my pleasure," Francis replied, pressing a

section of the wall next to a keycard box that was anchored there. "Have a productive trip."

A large section of the wall opposite the Deadhauls slid to one side, revealing another ramp.

"Let's get our guns," Rose said, turning on the truck and speeding out of The Morgue. "Time for a convoy!"

CHAPTER 27

"*B*radley, give me the status of the station," I said over my connector, once we were outside of The Morgue. *"Any more incoming?"*

"Hello, Chief," Bradley replied. *"We were surrounded by a large force of criminal elements. The Riders are still out there, but the rest of the gangs seemed to have received some signal and have left the perimeter."*

"Are you still on lockdown?"

"Partially, sir," Bradley said, hesitantly. *"I've managed to increase our numbers on the force somewhat, sir."*

"Excellent," I answered, relieved that the officer recruitment pool at the Academy had sent over new recruits. *"How many?"*

"We're currently at sixty-five percent operational," Bradley answered. *"I was informed the personnel that were hurt will be with the Medevacs for four to six weeks."*

"Sixty-five percent is good, but we need more," I pointed out. *"Even with minimal defenses, having the station at one-hundred percent is the goal."*

"Yes, sir," Bradley said. *"I do have some rather unconventional methods to increase our officers, but I would need your authorization to use that method."*

The Academy was moving too slowly. We needed those recruits now.

"Bradley, you do whatever is necessary to get those numbers where they need to be."

"Are you certain, Chief? I mean it is a bit unorthodox, but it will bring our numbers right up."

"Do it," I said. *"Call me when we're at one-hundred percent."*

"Will do, sir," Bradley said with increased energy. I could almost see the salute over the connector. *"I still feel uneasy with you and the team being out there. I could send a small force, now that we have some officers. Just as a precaution to help keep you all safe."*

"The offer is appreciated, but I don't want to risk it," I replied. *"Besides, we're moving to the wall and the neutral zone. I don't want any more PPD officers in harm's way."*

"Understood, sir," Bradley said. *"A word of advice, since I know you didn't really grow up in the Badlands—"*

"Excuse me?" I countered. *"I was born and raised in the Badlands."*

"Well, you were raised by valkyries, and no offense, but that's not really being raised in the Badlands," Bradley said. *"If the Badlands was a brawl in a bar, you would be the dragon outside looking at all the fighting going on."* He paused. *"Again, no offense."*

"Some taken," I said. *"What are you trying to say, Lieutenant? Spit it out."*

"Just that a dragon raised by valkyries wouldn't really know the difficulty of being raised in the Badlands."

"Have you ever eaten a dinner prepared by Hilda?"

"Can't say that I've had the honor, I'm sure it was—"

"Horrific at best, and damn near lethal at worst," I snapped, feeling the anger rise. *"Don't tell me about the difficulties of being raised in the Badlands until you've spent years surrounded by blood-thirsty women who would stab you several times just to say hello."*

"Sorry, sir," Bradley said. *"I overstepped my bounds."*

"Yes, you have," I said. *"Stick to getting that station filled and let me worry about the rest."*

There was some hesitation on the other side of the line. I had just ripped into the kid, but I was getting pretty tired of hearing how I didn't know anything about the Badlands. I caught it from all sides, especially my direct team, and I wasn't about to start accepting that level of personal criticism from *everyone* in the PPD.

"Again, sir," Bradley said, finally, *"my apologies. The reason I was making that reference is that there are some areas you want to steer clear of on your way to the wall and the neutral zone. I wasn't trying to question your upbringing, sir... much. I'm just suggesting you keep off the primary roads that lead to the Netherworld Proper."*

Bradley sounded sincere, making me feel like a dick.

Maybe I was being more of a hard-ass than I needed to be?

Ugh.

"Look, Bradley," I said with some effort, *"I'm under a fair bit of stress here, so take my outbursts with a grain of salt, okay?"*

"Yes, sir," he replied, his voice on the mend. *"I understand completely."*

"Good. Now, what do you suggest we should do as far as taking the roads less traveled?"

"Your best bets are Desolation View or Perdition Valley."

"And why is that, Lieutenant?" I asked, checking my datapad. *"I'm not seeing either of them on the map."*

"Lieutenant Blaze should know them," Bradley answered. *"Those roads are unused and mostly unknown. Both are a little out of the way. They're far enough from the city to be safe, but close enough to get you to the wall undetected."*

"Thank you, Bradley," I said, *"but a straight line is fastest. Time is a factor in getting these weapons."*

"Well," he argued, *"when the gangs were leaving the perimeter of the station, we overheard some of them say that they were heading back to the Strip and the outlying roads to intercept you."*

"You heard them say that?"

"Not in those exact words," Bradley answered. *"More like, 'back to the Strip so we can crush those fuckers before they get their hands on any weapons.'"*

"I see," I said, wondering how they were getting this information. *"Thank you for informing me, Lieutenant."*

"Just looking out for you, Chief," Bradley replied. *"We're the PPD. Death before Dismemberment...wait, that's not right. Give us liberty, then death?"*

"That doesn't sound quite—"

"I got it!" Bradley exclaimed. *"I regret I have only one life to give for the PPD, and it's yours."*

That couldn't be right, could it? If so, I was going to have to look into changing the Badlands PPD motto at my first convenience. Translation: I was never going to be changing that motto.

"Lieutenant?" I said, feeling even more tired than before.

"Yes, sir?"

"Keep the station safe until we get back."

"Yes, sir!"

I ended the call and glanced over at Rose. She was keeping pace with two Deadhauls in front of us. That was surprising, considering that cruise control wasn't something I'd put in her vocabulary.

"What did he say?" she asked, increasing speed, but not passing Graffon and Doe in Alpha Three. She was tailgating them, which seemed even dumber than when people do it during normal driving. So much for cruise control. "Did he get more personnel?"

"He did," I answered. "He also said the Strip is going to be crawling with criminals, ready to intercept us on our way to the wall."

"Shit," Rose said, tapping the onboard data system. "We're going to have to go off-road."

"He mentioned Desolation View or—"

"Perdition Valley?" Rose asked, tapping the screen and pressing send. The new options would be sent to the other Deadhauls. "How would he know about those roads?"

I gave her a look. "What are you saying?"

"Desolation View and Perdition Valley are old smuggling routes," Rose answered. "No one, except decrepit, broken-down criminals, would know about them."

169

Interesting.

It would explain why the roads weren't on the map. The smuggling part seemed to make sense, though, especially knowing that everyone in the Badlands was going to be gunning for our cargo.

"Are you a decrepit, broken-down criminal, Rose?" I asked, teasing.

"I'm not decrepit," she deadpanned.

I cracked a smile at that.

"Anyway, Bradley obviously knew the roads, but it does beg the question *how* he knew about them." I ran a finger along side the barrel of Pinky. "Maybe he has family who used to run the routes? Actually, maybe he has family who were in the PPD *stopping* smugglers?"

"Don't know," Rose answered. "It *is* a good idea to take the roads if the Strip is a gauntlet."

She tapped on Perdition Valley and pressed confirm. The route became highlighted on the map.

So much for going the straight and narrow.

We were taking the road to Perdition.

CHAPTER 28

*B*ernard had swerved over to the right and led the convoy into an uninhabited part of the Badlands. I didn't see any tumbleweeds or anything, but there were a few broken-down shanties and some rusted signs. Even the road, if you could call it that, had cracks and potholes all over the place. There were even full sections of the pavement gone, causing us to drive on dirt part of the time.

Honestly, though, this was the kind of place I could see calling home one day. Far away from the hustle and bustle of city life, but not so far that I couldn't drive in and grab supplies as needed.

Yeah, a guy could really stretch his wings out in this area of the Badlands.

Just as a bit of serenity filled my mind, the encrypted phone rang.

Rose connected the call and pressed speaker.

"This road sucks," Bernard stated. "I mean it makes sense to head through Perdition Valley, since no one has used this road for years, but it's also a road...inside...a... valley." He'd said the last three words in a sarcastic and staccato way. "Perfect for an ambush and shit, you know?"

Shit. I honestly hadn't considered that. Maybe I *was* a little too green about the way Badlanders thought. Valkyries would never ambush anyone. There was no honor in it, and that's precisely why I hadn't thought of it either.

Yep, I was definitely *not* as savvy as I'd thought, at least when it came to the ways people in this land processed the world. Specifically, the criminal element.

I glanced over at Rose and recalled the few adventures we'd had together.

Okay, so maybe not *just* the criminal element.

"What made you think to go this way?" Bernard asked.

"I didn't," Rose said. "One of our Lieutenants, Bradley, back at PPD HQ suggested it."

"You trust this Lieutenant?"

"Nope," Rose said immediately.

"Yes," I said, immediately afterward. "She doesn't trust anyone, Bernard."

"Nor should she," Bernard replied. "Misplaced trust is a recipe for death, and trust is always misplaced."

"Yep," agreed Rose. "It's why I'm still alive."

That was a pretty sour outlook on life. If you couldn't trust your partner on the force, who could you trust?

I gave another sidelong glance at Rose.

"Are you saying you don't trust me, Rose?"

"Not even a little bit, Chief," she replied. It wasn't a heartless response, just a direct one. "Can't afford to."

"Yeah?" I had to admit that her words stung a little. "Well, I don't trust you either."

"Wise," she replied with a nod. "I wouldn't trust me if I were you. That'd be suicide."

What?

"Chief," interjected Bernard, "has this Bradley guy saved your life?"

"No," I answered, finding the question odd.

"Has he taken a round meant for you? Suffered any injury or lost a limb defending you?"

At this point, I was just frowning at the phone, wondering what the hell he was talking about.

"No, Bernard," I answered in a sour tone, "I just met him earlier today, before we left the station."

There were a few moments of silence.

"Thorny?" Bernard sighed.

"What?"

"How has this Chief lasted this long? I mean, seriously, how is this dipshit still alive?"

Dipshit?

"Good question," Rose answered, glancing at me. "Luck, I guess. Ample doses of it, too. Of course, to be fair, he does have the best damn team in the Badlands PPD keeping his dragon ass alive."

Nice. Her words *did* convey one tidbit of selflessness, though.

"So you think Alpha Team is the best, eh?"

"Not at all."

I squinted. "But you said that I had the best team in the Badlands covering me."

"You do," she replied, giving me a quick look. "Me, Lethal Mercy, and Last Word."

I rolled my eyes at that. She *was* good, but not *that* good.

"This is a stupid route," Bernard stated, finally. "You may want to get your ass killed, but I'm still somewhat fond of breathing. Sending alternate."

A new line appeared on the map screen in the center of the dashboard. It was a quick right about a half-mile ahead.

It also seemed to cause Rose to catch her breath.

"You're fucking mental," she said, after a pause. "Graffon can't make those turns. We'll lose her Deadhaul and two of our team."

"Can she drift?" Bernard asked. "You must have taught her the basics, right?"

"Of course she can drift," Rose snapped. "I designed the offensive driving training for the Badlands PPD."

"Meaning *I* designed it via proxy," Bernard countered. "Then what's the issue? You scared, Thorny?"

"This isn't drifting on flat terrain," Rose said. "Deadman's Drift has sheer drops on most of the turns, it's downhill, and visibility is limited."

"Exactly," Bernard answered. "If you think I'm going to take a route suggested by a Lieutenant I don't even know, you're crazier than your Chief."

Rose's hands gripped the wheel so tight that here hands were turning white.

"There's a reason its called Deadman's Drift, Bernie."

"If you've kept up with your driving, this should be easier than wiping a hellion's ass," Bernard answered.

"If not, then you deserve to be at the bottom of the Drift."

She didn't reply as we approached the turn off.

"So, what exactly is this Deadman's Drift?" I asked, not liking the idea of falling off the edge of a cliff.

"Just another road," she grumbled. "Well, more like a training ground for hellions."

"For hellions?" I gulped. "So, it's suicidal?"

"Something like that," Rose said, shaking her head. "Deadman's Drift is several miles of downhill terrain, formed of hairpin turns. You can't take the turns normally. You have to drift into them and slide your way out. Every turn has a sheer drop off." She paused as her voice grew distant. "You miss the turn..."

"You end your drift at the bottom of the canyon," Bernard finished.

"Sounds suicidal, all right," I said. "Have you done this Drift, Rose?"

She nodded. "Several times actually. Just not in a Deadhaul. We're going to have to adjust the steering if we're doing this, Bernie."

"We'll stop at the entrance," he replied. "You can brief the team and make the adjustments. If you trained them, they should be fine; if not—natural selection. Besides, this is the fastest way to the wall."

Bernard ended the call.

"Well, isn't he just full of compassion?" I said.

"He's a hellion, compassion isn't part of the package."

She had a tendency of saying things like that, but I'd seen her merciful side. It usually was of the type where she killed someone quickly instead of making it drawn out and torturous, but, for a hellion, that was saying something.

"Do you think Graffon can handle this?" I asked.

"She's the most solid driver on the team," Rose answered. "If anyone can do it, besides Bernie and me, of course, it's her. She's fearless."

I nodded as the vehicles took the turn off and slowed down to a stop.

"Is he right?" I asked, looking at the landscape ahead. "Is this the fastest way to the wall?"

She shoved the Deadhaul into park and gave me a sobering look.

"Only if we make it out alive."

CHAPTER 29

We sat at the entrance of Deadman's Drift, where the insanity of hellions was instantly reinforced. I looked over the edge and saw the bottom of the valley, several kilometers below us.

I kept Pear in the Deadhaul.

Last thing I needed was him flinging himself off the edge and flying around. I wouldn't try that descent, even with my wings out. The currents of air racing across the side of the cliff were intense. Thermals raced past us with colder cross-currents shifting the direction of the wind. If I tried to fly down the road, I'd end up slamming into the cliff face several times.

Bernard was under a Deadhaul, adjusting the steering for the upcoming descent into madness. Rose was having a conversation with Graffon, probably about the joys and intricacies of near-death driving.

Butch, Doe, and Silk stood near the edge shaking their heads.

"No guardrails on the turns," Butch said.

"Noticed that, did you," I said. "No guard rails anywhere on this suicide run."

"We're going down that?" Silk asked with a grunt. "Why don't we all just jump over the edge now? Save us the trouble of having to drive to our deaths."

"Can these vehicles even navigate those turns?" Doe added, looking back at the Deadhauls. "They can't be taken normally. The road is barely wide enough for cars, let alone those monsters."

There was no arguing with that. "Rose says we have to 'drift' them."

"Oh," Doe answered in his usual emotionless voice. "Drift these turns? In armored trucks designed for anything but a drift? I see."

"We're all going to die," Silk moaned. "This is the end."

I grimaced at him. "I thought Rose designed the offensive drivers training course for the PPD?"

"Of course she did," Doe answered. "Doesn't mean we were insane enough to take that course." He tilted his head toward my second-in-command. "*Rose* was leading the course. You've driven with her. Two and two, Chief."

"Did *any* of you take it?" I asked, realizing that the chances of dying in a fiery crash at the bottom of the valley had just multiplied.

"Graffon did," Silk replied.

"I mean *besides* Graffon."

"Nope," said Silk. "Graffon's the only one who is just as batshit crazy as the Lieutenant." He peered at me. "Haven't you noticed?"

"Stop pissing your panties, pixie," Bernard said, from behind us. I turned to see him wiping the grease from his hands. "We'll get down this valley one way or another."

"Oh, well, *now* I'm full of confidence," Silk droned. "And I'm not a pixie, you dick surfer. You're worse than Rose."

"Thank you," Bernard said with a bow. It was clearly a mock bow, especially with the look of disappointment he was wearing. "You're all supposed to be the fearsome Badlands PPD. Why are you scared of a little hill?"

"That isn't a hill," Doe replied, still looking down the cliff. "It's a mountain, leading into a valley."

"One man's hill is another's mountain," Bernard said, jumping back under the Deadhaul for a second. He then slid back out, holding a freshly retrieved wrench while dusting himself off. "This is the fastest route to the wall... that isn't an ambush."

He headed off to the second Deadhaul to adjust the steering. I followed him. He slid under the truck and began tinkering on the driver's side.

I crouched down and pulled out my datapad, checking the map of the area. That's when I realized that even though this was a winding road with treacherous turns, it did lead straight to the wall and the neutral zone. I was mostly surprised it was even on the map.

"You really think the other roads are an ambush?" I asked. "Bradley *is* one of us."

"How long have you been the chief, Phoenix?" he scoffed. "Two...three weeks?"

"Almost three weeks," I answered. "What does that have to do with—?"

"So you're three weeks in, and you're willing to trust a

lieutenant—that you met just earlier today, mind you—with your life?"

"He's a PPD officer," I stated. "He knows—"

"More importantly," Bernard interrupted, "are you willing to trust this Bradley with the lives of your team... and your weird-ass little brother?"

I held my ground. "Lieutenant Bradley is a PPD officer. He would never betray the shield."

"Would never betray the..." Bernard laughed heartily for a few seconds. "Were you raised by hippies or something?"

"Valkyries."

"Oh, that's right," he continued laughing. "Even worse." There was a cranking sound as Bernard grunted, obviously working a bolt free. "Do you know how many government officials I bought back in my day, Phoenix?"

"Many, I would guess."

It was meant as a dig. Bernard, of course, took it as a compliment.

"*Very* many." Another grunt. "Now, Phoenix, use your poor excuse for a brain for just a second here. Do you *seriously* think the Badlands PPD is any different when it comes to taking bribes?"

Again, I held my ground. "Yes, I absolutely believe that."

"Why?" he laughed again, pointing a wrench at me. "Just because you're the chief?" I held my response, so he continued. "Oh, come on! You can't possibly be this naive. Were you even raised in the Badlands?"

I closed my eyes and gritted my teeth.

"Yes," I said slowly. "I was raised in the Badlands."

"Then you should know the basic tenet that *every* kid is taught from day one: you trust no one. That goes double for anyone who could profit from your death."

"Bradley wouldn't profit..." Rose's words came back to me: *"You know, if we don't make it back, he becomes the next Chief. A denizen of hell is next in line."*

"That look is telling me you're starting to put it together," Bernard said. "And here I was, starting to think that your head might be filled with rat shit." He peered up at me. "It's common for dragons to be a bit stupid about things like this, you know." He shrugged. "Doesn't matter anyway, I guess. We'll find out soon enough."

"What do you mean?"

"Desolation View and Perdition Valley are both closer to Infernal City than here," Bernard answered, pointing back the way we came. "We should've been on one of those by now. If there were ambushes waiting for us—"

"They would've intercepted us by now," I interrupted, making the connection. "When we don't show up, we'll know the full breadth of our situation."

"Maybe there's some legit gray matter in that ball of rock you call a head, after all, Phoenix," Bernard stated. "If your Bradley knew about those two roads, he'll figure out what we're up to shortly. That means we'll be having company soon. Unless, like you said, he's PPD, he would never betray the shield."

I held my intended response back.

Regardless of what Bernard...*and* Rose thought, I wasn't going to give up on Lieutenant Bradley just yet. He seemed like a decent kid, and he'd already jumped the numbers in the PPD by a decent margin. I wasn't sure what his 'unorthodox methods' consisted of to get even more officers, but his willingness to show initiative was excellent. Or, at least had been up until the negative conversations I'd had with a couple of lovely hellions.

Damnit.

"How long before all the vehicles are adjusted?" I asked.

"Now you're thinking," Bernard said, grinning. "Fifteen minutes…ten, if you stop your gabbing."

"Make it eight," I commanded, doing my best to get the upper hand, "and lets get the hell out of here."

CHAPTER 30

I kept my eyes on the horizon.

If Bernard was right, and my intuition was telling me he was, we were going to be joined by several groups out to eliminate us. I didn't want to be standing around like a target when they arrived. Dragons have enhanced vision, which I used to scan the area behind us...nothing yet.

Rose had finished her conversation with Graffon and was heading back.

I still had a hard time thinking Bradley would betray us. It would mean that he was working for someone who wanted to destroy the PPD.

"I've been thinking," I said.

"Don't strain that one brain cell," she retorted. "You may need it later."

"I think you missed your calling," I said. "I'm sure hellion comedy would be a huge draw, oh except for that part where you'd shoot the hecklers."

She nodded, as if giving it thought.

"Hecklers? Who would be that suicidal?"

"Good point," I acquiesced. "Anyway, I think we have a problem."

"You mean besides the fact that every criminal is after us," she started, "we have no weapons except what we we're wearing or stealing, and now we're going to drift down what's possibly the most dangerous road in the entire Badlands?"

"Yes, besides that," I said, after a pause. "I think we have a mole in the PPD."

"A mole?" Rose asked, cocking her head to one side. "Are you sure?"

"I have a suspicion that—"

"What part of 'trust no one' don't you understand?" she interrupted. "Of course there's a mole. Probably several." She snorted. "What is wrong with you? A few weeks ago everyone was trying to erase your ass, most of them still are."

"Eraseyourass," yipped Pear with a laugh.

"Well, but, you said—"

"Wake the fuck up, Chief," Rose blurted.

"Fuckupfuckupfuckup," cackled Pear.

"*Trust no one*. That needs to be your default MO." She nodded at the rearview mirror. "You see our team?"

I turned back to see the rest of the team getting into the Deadhauls.

"Yes, I see them," I said. "You *trust* them?"

"Fu...fudge no," she said, changing her expletive mid-stride to avoid giving Pear another reason to burst out in song. She was shaking her head at me. "This is the Badlands. I *trust* no one, but I *tolerate* them. If they were to turn on me, I would offer them the chance to provide an explanation...*before* I shot them."

"That's you being generous?"

"Fu...fudge, yes. Anyone else, I'd just shoot. No explanation necessary."

My brain understood that she was right. It was an important survival tactic that I was slowly coming to grips with here in the Badlands, but we couldn't operate the PPD that way. We needed to be able to count on each other when the fan and the shit were one.

"We have to change that," I stated, after a pause. "The PPD can't—"

"The PPD is corrupt like most every other criminal organization in the Badlands," Rose stopped me as she started up the Deadhaul and looked toward the horizon. "We just get to wear badges."

Regardless of what she or Bernard thought, I had to believe that there were solid officers in the PPD. And even more to the point, I knew damn well that Rose was one of them. Sure, she was filled to the brim with bravado, and she loved being an asshole whenever the opportunity presented itself—which seemed incredibly often—but she *was* a good cop. Rough around the edges, definitely, but also trustworthy as hell.

Maybe it was just my valkyrie upbringing, but I had no option but to believe it.

"Not *everyone* in the PPD is corrupt."

"Everyone has a price, Chief," Rose sighed. "Sometimes it's money, sometimes it's favors or prestige. But everyone has a price."

"What's yours, then?"

"What?" Rose asked, turning to me suddenly. "My *what?*"

"Price," I said. "You said everyone has a price, right? That must include you, right?"

"Fuck you," she said with a growl.

"Fuckyoufuckyoufuckyou," sang Pear.

"Shi...shingles," Rose hissed. "Alpha Team is the exception, Chief. I picked and vetted them myself. I've tested them, and even had my people try and bribe them. Every single one of them is clean. Crazy as fu...fudge, but clean."

"But you don't trust them," I noted. "The team *you* picked?"

"Now you're getting it," she answered. "I'm a hellion. Most days I don't trust myself not to shoot everyone around me, just for some peace and quiet. They're clean now, but anyone can become dirty, if the price is right. Each member of Alpha has been given the opportunity for some seriously high bribes, though, so let's say that I'm cautiously optimistic about them."

I nodded. It wasn't much, but it was something.

"What about me?" I asked. "You think I'm corrupt too?"

"If I did, we wouldn't be having this conversation," Rose replied. "I tried to dust you on principle, not your morals. You're the new chief after all. If you were any cleaner, I'd have to call you soap."

"That makes me feel better," I said. "You were trying to kill me because it's tradition."

"Glad that's clear."

I smiled and nodded. "And the rest of the PPD? Are they all corrupt? Besides Alpha, I mean."

"I didn't pick the rest of the PPD," Rose replied. "As far as I know, they all work for Masters or some other criminal."

"Fuck that," I said, angrily. "The PPD *will* uphold the law while I'm Chief."

"Fuckthatfuckthatfuckthat...weeeeee!"

"You don't get it," she said, adjusting her seat and wheel position, obviously prepping for the drive down the hill. "Why do you think we have everyone after us? *You* upheld the law. Now the Badlands evolutionary equivalent of natural selection is on its way to correct your behavior." She paused and gave me a look. "Do you really want a clean PPD?"

"Yes, I do," I replied without hesitation. "A PPD that will never betray the badge."

"Then you'll have to clean house...top to bottom."

I furrowed my brow. "What are you talking about?"

"Remember that mole you thought we had?" she asked.

"Yes, I have a feeling it's—"

"Lieutenant Bradley?"

"How did you know I was going to say him?"

"Look," Rose said, pointing behind us. "Who suggested Desolation View or Perdition Valley?"

"Bradley," I answered, "but we didn't take either of those."

"I know," Rose said, starting the engine. "There are only three main smuggling routes to the wall and the neutral zone, those two and this one. No one is crazy enough to take this one."

"Except us," I said. "And...anyone waiting to ambush us at the other two routes."

"See?" she said with an evil smile. "I told you that remaining brain cell would come in handy sooner or later."

I could see the plumes of dust in the distance.

They were coming.

CHAPTER 31

"*We'll be using two minute gaps,*" Rose directed over the connector. "*Alpha Two will set the pace. Alpha Three...Graffon, you'll maintain a two minute distance. Any closer and you'll drive into the tire wake of the vehicle in front of you. Your visibility will be zero, resulting in your next turn being your last. We'll be two minutes behind you.*"

There was a brief cough over the connector.

Rose gave me a look and rolled her eyes.

"*Sorry,*" she breathed, "*Dark Succubus will be maintaining Alpha Three two minutes behind Bernard.*"

"*Roger that, Bloody Rose,*" Graffon answered, her voice holding a tinge of excitement. "*Two minutes and we burn rubber on the slide—ass first.*"

"*We run silent to the bottom, unless there's an emergency,*" Rose answered. "*Let's keep the distractions down to nil.*"

Rose turned the connector off.

"Bloody Rose?" I asked, holding back a grin.

"She insisted on it and was about to get into the BTU

189

code of conduct," Rose answered with a sigh. "I figured it was less painful to agree to the handle than listen to an hour of BTU regulations."

"I understand," I said, nodding. "Is that your trucker handle, or is that what we're calling you now?"

Rose ignored me for a second as she flexed her jaw muscles, keeping an eye on the Deadhaul in front of her.

"I'd give you the answer you deserve," Rose said under her breath, "but the little echo chamber that is your brother would spend the whole way down repeating it."

"Also," I pressed because...well, why not?, "are *you* the bloody Rose or is the bloody part how you leave others after they prick their hands on your thorny thorns? Just curious."

"Chief," She rasped, giving me a one finger salute without looking my way, "bury that so far up that you can't sit for a week."

I grinned and then looked out of the passenger side window. Our retirement committee was advancing.

"They're almost on top of us," I pointed out. "This is going to be tight."

"That's what she said," Rose snapped with a grin of her own.

That's when I knew two things: We'd probably make it down the mountain mostly intact, and I was going to wish I had spread my wings, jumped over the edge, and taken my chances with the thermals.

Looking down was *not* the best idea.

I gulped.

"When was the last time you drifted down this road, again?"

"Too long ago for me to recall," she answered. "Don't worry though, it's just like getting shot at."

"What?"

"It's not the shooting that kills you—it's the impact of the rounds."

"What kind of twisted—?"

"Come on. *Everyone* knows that saying."

"Must be a hellion thing." I said.

"And your mom never said anything like that...right?"

"Valkyries do have something similar, now that I think of it: a swinging blade doesn't kill you until it does."

"Exactly," Rose said with a nod. She tightened her grip on the steering wheel as Bernard's Deadhaul took off with a screech and a growl. "Valkyries know their shit."

"No," I replied, wringing my hands together, "it only means hellions and valkyries are both insane."

"Knowtheirshitknowtheirshit—"

"Pear," Rose said, her voice a gentle menace, "do not repeat my words and sit quietly."

"Yes, Rose," he said in a calm voice.

I turned to find him sitting back, his hands clasped on his lap. He was silent and sat still. Only Hilda could get a similar response from Pear.

Impressive.

Bragons clearly responded to the potential promise of pain.

"That's a good bragon," Rose replied without looking back. "Now find the harness and strap in. We're going to have a fun ride down the slide."

"Fun ride down the slide, weeeeeee!"

I heard the center latch of the heavy duty X-harness click closed.

"How the hell—?"

"Ninety seconds until Alpha Three heads down," Rose said, glancing at me. "You may want to tighten that harness, Chief. Like painted-on pants tight. Don't need you sliding all over the place."

I pulled on the straps that tightened my X-harness to make sure I was secured. I followed Alpha Two with my gaze as they approached the first of the many turns. The road was barely wide enough for the Deadhaul.

Drifting is a technique in which the driver of a vehicle briefly oversteers at the start of a turn, causing the rear of the vehicle to enter a controlled lateral skid until the turn is complete. Deadman's Drift required a driver to basically laterally skid his way down the face of a cliff, on a road carved out of turns too tight to be taken any other way.

The vehicles we were driving were not designed to drift.

They were especially not designed to drive down a hellion mountain road of death.

What I was looking at was impossible.

That didn't stop Bernard from taking the first turn at speed. He raced for it, and at the last second cut the wheel to the right, forcing the rear of the Deadhaul to slide sideways. When it looked like the truck was about to go over the edge, he cut the wheel in the opposite direction and sped into the next turn, leaving a cloud of smoke in his wake as the tires burned.

Graffon waited a minute more while stepping on the

accelerator. Her Deadhaul's engine screamed with a roar and lurched forward as she followed. Rose stepped on the accelerator and the engine of our Deadhaul growled like an angry beast.

I glanced back, noticing the plume of smoke getting closer. It wasn't one vehicle, but rather a fleet of mixed and matched vehicles, ranging from large trucks to sleek supercars. The large trucks were never going to make it down the road. Some of the smaller trucks had a chance if they drove so slowly that it would be faster to walk down.

The only vehicles that stood a chance were the sleek supercars speeding our way. Unless they were being driven by trained maniacs, I had the feeling most of those supercars were going to be wrecks at the bottom of the cliff.

"Let's see how the Dark Succubus handles the first turn," Rose said under her breath as she clenched the wheel even tighter.

Despite all her talk, I knew that deep down, Rose cared for Alpha Team. She'd never admit it out loud, but her actions demonstrated how concerned she was for Graffon in this moment.

"Rose?"

"Shut it," she shot back, her eyes riveted on Alpha Three. "I need to see how she takes this turn."

"It's just that some of these vehicles are getting close—"

"Don't care," she snapped. "If Graffon fails this first turn, she's done. We're sweeping up Doe and her team from the ground below."

She had a point, and the drivers behind us had guns.

"Just thought—"

"Don't. Deadhauls are almost everything proof. Alpha Three is my priority right now. Should be yours, too."

I looked down the road to see the speeding Deadhaul.

Graffon raced into the first turn, and for a second I thought she was going to sail off the side of the cliff. At the last possible moment, she turned the wheel hard, causing the rear of the Deadhaul to slide into the turn. Just when it looked like she would slam into the cliffside, she pulled the wheel in the opposite direction, executing a perfect drift.

It was flawless.

"Well, damn," Rose said with admiration. "That was one hell of a drift."

"This is Dark Succubus!" Graffon's voice came over the group channel. *"I got the metal to the pedal and the thing to the floor! Let's go, Bloody Rose, get your fat ass moving!"*

"I said run silent and I meant it," Rose answered in mock anger. *"You have a problem following orders?"*

She was actually smiling like a kid at Deathmas, which was a little known holiday where valkyries allowed kids to be rambunctious without fear of repercussion. That holiday only came once every five years, and it only applied to you if you were under twenty…or if you were a bragon.

"I'm sorry Lieutenant," Graffon answered quickly. *"I didn't mean—"*

"That…was an excellent drift though, Dark Succubus," Rose said with a grin. *"You have a mountain full of them. Keep your eyes on the road. We're right behind you. Bloody Rose out."*

CHAPTER 32

*G*unfire raced across the side of our Deadhaul.

"What the hell, Chief?" Rose said, racing down the road. "You didn't think it was important to let me know how close these idiots were?"

"Are you joking right now?" I asked, pulling out Pinky. "What do you think I was trying to tell you earlier?"

"You're the chief," Rose said, speeding down the straightaway that led to the first turn. "You really need to work on your communication skills."

Two of the supercars were right behind us, firing guns. The road was too narrow for them, and they had to chase us in single file. I opened the plexan window and undid my harness. I leaned out of the window and fired Pinky. There was almost no chance of hitting the lead car in pursuit, but I didn't need to hit him. I just needed to throw off their approach to the turn.

The dragon round hit the road and exploded, causing the pursuers to swerve around the small crater I created.

Fortunately for them, the road here was still wide enough to allow for swerving.

"That should do it," I said, strapping in and closing the window.

They hadn't waited two minutes. This meant they were right behind us as Rose slid into the first turn. The burning rubber of the tires threw up a cloud of smoke, obscuring everything behind us.

For half-a-second, it looked like we were going to be the first airborne Deadhaul.

Rose slammed the wheel to one side and skirted the inside of the turn. If Graffon's drift was flawless, Rose's execution made Graffon look like an amateur.

The first supercar realized the upcoming turn a few seconds too late and sailed off the edge of the cliff. The second car tried to course correct.

As if driving this treacherous hill wasn't insane enough, Rose deftly lowered her window, drew Lethal Mercy, and fired, hitting the second supercar...all while keeping the Deadhaul securely in its lane.

The driver swerved to avoid the gunfire. He must have miscalculated the width of the road, and suddenly found himself midair—following the first car.

"Showoff," I choked, freaked out over how smooth that entire motion had been for her.

Rose was one deadly woman.

"That won't stop them," she said, holstering her gun.

She was right.

One look in the side mirror told me that more vehicles were racing down the cliff. Apparently, some of these criminals were as crazy as hellions and knew how to drift.

We needed to slow them down.

"You'd better grab one of the mini guns," Rose said, proving that we were of the same mind.

"And do what?" I asked. "Fire out of the window while you're drifting all over the place?" I gulped. "Weren't you the one who told me to strap myself in tighter?"

"Back door," Rose said, drifting into another turn. "Gun ports. Mini-gun in gun port and pull trigger? You want me to drive and shoot?"

"You just did," I reminded her.

"That's only because I'm phenomenal," Rose answered, "but the turns get tighter, and the body gets fatigued. I can't keep doing that, which means you're going to have to convince the bad guys that chasing us on this cliff is a bad idea. I'm going to need to focus."

She was being glib, but I could see the thin sheen of sweat on her brow, and for the first time since I met her, I was concerned. Rose never sweat and never lost her composure. What I heard in her voice was fear. Not because we were being chased, it was the cliff itself.

"Got it," I said. The next turn was up ahead, about a quarter of a mile. I unstrapped, climbed over the small passenger area, and jumped to the spacious cargo area of the Deadhaul.

"Hello, Zeezee," Pear said as I passed by him.

"Uh…hi," I replied.

It was incredibly odd seeing him so well-behaved.

I shook my head and got into position.

"Okay," I called out, "you get us to the bottom in one piece, and I'll work on explaining the error of chasing the Badlands PPD."

"Appreciate it."

I looked for a strap or something to hold on to as she suddenly drifted into another turn.

I rolled around the back, slamming into the floor, and bouncing off the side with a grunt.

"A little warning next time?"

"Sorry about that," she yelled back. "Turn!"

"Haha, hilarious," I said. "We just—"

I stumbled forward, headlong into the side of the truck again as she executed another drift. She navigated the turn expertly, of course, but the maneuver was too extreme to remain in place without being thrown around.

I pressed Whoosh and formed my scales. My wings spread out, too large for the interior of the Deadhaul. I pressed them against the sides of the truck, keeping myself in place.

Better than nothing.

I picked up one of the mini-guns and slid over to the rear gun port. Thin slats covered in plexan rested above larger slats designed to fire weapons through.

My first thought was, why would Francis need gun ports in Deadhauls?

"How many?" Rose yelled from the front.

"Too many to count," I yelled back. "They aren't close. The turns are slowing them down, but they're coming."

"Time to thin the herd a bit," Rose said. "Hit the lead cars and cause blockage. The road is too narrow for them to get around. That, and the drifts should buy us enough time to get to the wall first."

I propped the mini-gun in the port and opened fire. The gun shredded the lead vehicles, removing the entire front end of one of the cars. I nodded with satisfaction as they screeched to a stop behind us.

"That seemed to have—shit!"

"What?" Rose asked. "Turn! Never mind...I see them."

One of the larger vehicles in the pursuit group was barreling down the road, clearing a path for the others. Cars and trucks were being pushed out of the way and over the side of the cliff. Some of the drivers were able to escape the sweep, but others weren't that lucky.

"What kind of truck is that...and how is it managing the turns?"

"That's a Hellion Sweeper," Rose answered in a worried voice. "Whoever is driving that thing is good... better than good." She followed that up with a barely audible, "How did they get a Sweeper? This complicates things."

She looked out of the window and then glanced back at me.

"No, shit," I said, watching the truck slam into everything in its way and closing. "It's getting closer."

"Shitshitshit," sang Pear in a quiet, almost reverent voice.

Weird.

"Change of plans," Rose said. "How strong are your wings?"

"Is this the time to be asking questions about my—?"

"Do you want to survive this little trip down the mountain?" she barked, taking another turn. "Or do you want to die when we're pushed off?"

"Non-death, thank you."

"Then answer the fu...fudging question! How strong are they?"

I opened fire on the Hellion Sweeper, but the front of the vehicle was covered in some kind of armor.

"Strong, fireproof, and covered in scales," I yelled back, feeling just as anxious as she felt. "I don't know what you're asking, specifically Rose. You've seen what my wings can do."

"Would they be strong enough to carry me and your brother to Alpha Three?"

"What?" I blurted. "No! I mean...I don't know. Maybe? But that would mean we are *outside* of this Deadhaul."

"Nothing gets past you," Rose snarked. "Stop wasting ammo. We need something stronger to stop that Sweeper."

"If you have any rockets in your pockets, toss them back here."

"I have something better than a rocket."

I furrowed my brow as the Sweeper edged closer to us. "What do you have that's better than a rocket...and why the hell didn't you give me that first?"

"Because it's a one-time use kind of weapon."

"What in the nine levels are—?" My blood froze. "You didn't?"

"I did," she replied, her eyes meeting mine in the rearview mirror. "You have to agree, a bomb is better than a rocket."

"Fuck me."

"Fuckmefuckmefuckmefuckme," Pear sang, a fair bit louder this time. 'Fuck' was his trigger word. "ZeeZeefuckmefuckmefuckme!"

"Pear," I said, trying to mimic Rose's tone from earlier, "not now."

He looked at me and began yelling. "Fuckmenowfuck-menowfuckmenownownnowowowowNOW!!"

"Pear, stop." Rose commanded and he grew silent. Annoying. "Let's go, Chief. We have to do this."

"Seriously? I mean…" I glanced ahead at the road, which was closing in on another turn, and then back at the oncoming Sweeper. "Seriously?"

"Dead serious," she said, navigating another turn. "Get moving. We're running out of time."

I stared at her, and she motioned for me to get on with it. I realized that 'insane' isn't the correct word to describe hellions. Hellions are *beyond* insane.

"What do you want me to do with this?" I said, holding up the mini-gun. "It's not like I have bottomless pockets in this jacket."

She accelerated to the next turn, putting some distance between us and the Sweeper. She drifted through and stopped. I made my way to the passenger seat with a lurch.

"Toss me the mini-gun and get to the front," she commanded, reaching back, unstrapping Pear, and grabbing him with one arm. "Self-destruct in thirty seconds."

CHAPTER 33

"You want us to jump down the side of the cliff?"

"No," Rose answered, jumping out of the Deadhaul, "I want you to jump to Alpha Three. Can you do it?"

"Do I have a choice?"

"Good point," she said with a nod. "We'd better go. We have about fifteen seconds, and we need to be out of the blast range." She gave me a hard look. "Ready?"

We stepped to the edge of the road, and I folded my wings.

"This is a bad idea."

"A bad idea is standing here talking about it," Rose said. "You hear that?"

It was the rumble of the Sweeper.

"Sweeper?"

"No, death," she retorted. "Once it makes that turn, it will slam into the Deadhaul. It will explode. Along with the road, and us, if we aren't off this cliff when that happens."

I grabbed her by the waist and made sure Pear was secure in my other arm.

With a grunt and a small prayer to anything that might be listening, I opened my wings and stepped off the edge. We glided for a few meters until the first crosswind. It pushed us hard into a dive.

Ten seconds later, an explosion rocked the cliff, sending rocks and debris in every direction.

"Boomboomboomboom!" yelled Pear. "Zeezeeboomboom!"

I couldn't focus on Pear because the wind pressing down on us wasn't letting me pull out of the dive. We were too heavy, and I had little maneuverability.

"It's no good," I managed. "We're too heavy. If we impact at this velocity, we're done."

"There," Rose said, pointing. "Alpha Three. Get me ahead of it, and then let me go."

"No! Are you trying to get yourself killed?"

"If you don't we all die," she said her voice hard. "Just ahead of it, before the next turn."

She was right. It was all I could do to angle us in the direction of Alpha Three. I banked with the wind behind me. Graffon was about to execute her next turn, when Rose pushed off me.

"ByebyeRosebyebye!" Pear yelled as Rose descended on the Deadhaul, just as Graffon slowed down to make the drift. "RosecanflyRosecanfly!"

"No she just falls...with style," I told him, pulling away to avoid the cliff wall.

She landed on the roof of the Deadhaul with a thud, nearly sliding off. She grabbed the edge of the beast at the last moment, and then managed to crawl to the passenger side. Doe must have seen it was her because he opted not to shoot first.

"I'm good, Chief," I heard Rose say in my connector. *"See if you can catch up with Bernard. I'll meet you at the bottom."*

"Hold on tight, Pear. We need to get to the ground."

"Weee!"

CHAPTER 34

The thermals and wind-shear were kicking my ass.

As bad as it was, though, I didn't want to consider Hilda's wrath if something happened to Pear.

If I went full dragon, my scales would protect me, even though we were probably too high to experiment with that theory. Pear, being half-dragon and half werebear, transformed into something with fur, not scales. Fur wasn't very good at dealing with falls from height. Not even bragon fur.

I shoved that thought out of my mind, and looked to see if I could locate Alpha Two.

Bernard was six minutes ahead of us and traveling around thirty kilometers per hour, which meant he had covered close to three kilometers in distance. I looked down the side of the cliff, locating his exact position.

I was getting tired from fighting with the cross currents. If I didn't find a way to get out of the wind, I would fatigue and be introduced to the ground…hard.

Hilda's words came back to me...the ones she said right before the first time she launched me off Heaven's Fang: *"It's not the falling that kills you, it's the sudden stop. Fall and die or fly and live. Choose."*

I forced my wings into a streamlined configuration and aimed for Alpha Two.

The wind buffeted us and pushed me off course a few times, but I corrected the angle of interception. That's when I realized I was coming in too low. I wasn't going to be able to pull off a graceful roof landing like Rose.

"Butch," I said over the connector, *"I'm going to need you to open the backdoor."*

"Sorry, Chief?" Butch replied.

"I need you to open your backdoor."

"Uh..." Butch started. *"Listen, Chief, I really respect you, and even like you...as a Chief. But you're not really my type. I mean—"*

"Open the back door of the Deadhaul, Butch!" I yelled. *"Open it now!"*

"Oh! I thought you meant—"

"Now!"

I approached the truck just as Bernard pulled out of a drift. One second earlier or later and I would have slammed into the side of the Deadhaul.

The back door flung open. Butch was standing in the opening like a large Malkyrie target.

I wrapped my wings around Pear and aimed my body to take most of the impact.

A second later, I slammed into Butch and launched him further into the Deadhaul.

Dragons may be thin, but our bodies are dense.

"What the fresh hell is this?" Silk yelled as I oriented myself. "Why are you here?"

"Thorny detonated the Deadhaul, didn't she?" Bernard called back from the front. It was obviously a rhetorical question. "Good girl. Did she make it?"

I thought I heard a tinge of concern in his voice.

"Yes," I answered. "She's Rose. Only thing I've seen tougher than her is a dragon."

"She's tougher than a dragon," Bernard countered, adding, "Present company included."

I ignored the insult, though he was probably right.

Butch shook off the impact and closed the backdoor with a slam. Malkyries were easily as tough as hellions.

"How...how'd you know she would pull something like that, Bernard?" I asked, dematerializing my wings. "Even I didn't see that coming, and I was in the Deadhaul with her."

"You were in the truck with her, true," Bernard answered, "but I'm in her head. I trained her to be one of best. What she did was the smartest course of action. Overwhelming odds, one approach, cut your losses and take down as many as you can."

"Again!" Pear yelled. "Againagainagainagain! Can we do it again, ZeeZee?"

Bernard whistled, clicked, and growled.

Pear instantly quieted and moved to sit in the corner, hands on his lap. Either I was going to learn to be as menacing as a hellion, or I had to learn to speak bragon.

I took inventory of the pain embracing my body and shook my head.

"No, Pear," I said, weary from the emergency exit from my Deadhaul. "ZeeZee needs to rest his head."

"That explosion?" Butch asked. "Was that your Deadhaul?"

I nodded. "Rose felt it was the best course of action, considering we were about to be squashed by something called a Sweeper."

"A Hellion Sweeper?" Bernard asked.

"Yes, big truck, armored, drifts the corners of this cliff like nothing."

"Well, slap me with a mace, and stab me twice," Bernard said. "Who the fuck did you piss off, exactly?"

"Everyone?" I answered and rested my head on the floor of the Deadhaul. "How soon to the wall and neutral zone."

"They won't be after us for about a day, since Thorny exploded the road, but we can't slow down," Bernard answered. "Not if they have a Sweeper."

"*Had* a Sweeper," I corrected him. "Rose blew it up, remember?"

"She blew up one of them," argued Bernard. "They never travel alone."

"Oh."

"The wall is about two hours away," Butch noted, looking at his datapad, "if we run into more trouble. Once there, we'll have to face them in the Desolate Flats. That won't be fun."

"Especially with Sweepers on our ass," agreed Bernard.

"What's the big deal about the Sweeper?" I asked. "It's just a big truck. Bulletproof, yes, but still just a truck."

"Not exactly," Bernard said after a pause, his jaw set.

"Sweepers lets us know that one of the hellion Houses is involved. Since you aren't that much of a target, even being the PPD Chief, that can only mean one thing."

"They know you're here," I stated as Butch directed me to one of the harnesses in the back. I wish I'd seen those when Rose had been driving our Deadhaul. Pear snapped his in place and tightened it without even being told to do it. Amazing. "What do you think the hellions want with you? To say hello?"

"Hellions don't forgive or forget, Phoenix," Bernard answered, taking another turn and drifting. Thankfully, the harnesses kept us all from rolling around. "They've come to finish what I started."

"Never a dull moment," I said, rubbing my temples. "I'm just going to rest my eyes for a second."

CHAPTER 35

"Switch to solar," I heard Bernard say. "We'll conserve the fuel for the return trip."

"Where are we?" I asked, shifting to get a better look. "There's a lot of...nothing."

"Desolate Flats," Bernard answered. "Wall and neutral zone is straight that way. We should get there in about thirty."

"I've been out for ninety minutes?"

"My guess is you bailed from your Deadhaul, carried Rose to Alpha Three, and then intercepted us, right?" Bernard asked. "You looked like you overextended yourself, buttercup. Winds in this valley can be a bitch. Your body just needed some downtime. Must be a dragon thing. I've seen it before."

"I've never had that happen," I rasped. "My body just shut down?"

"Don't stress it, stronger dragons than you have crashed and burned on this cliff," Bernard pointed out. "You were lucky your little brother acted as ballast. If you hadn't had his extra weight, you'd be smeared dragon right now."

I looked over at Pear, who was quietly sleeping. These were the only moments he was truly still and quiet, except when Rose or Bernard gave him shit, anyway. His face was so relaxed and peaceful. I shook my head and sniffed. Even though he was a tremendous pain in the ass, he was my little brother and I...cared for him. Man, that was hard to admit. Regardless of my feelings, I needed to make sure he got back to Hilda in one piece, or I would end up in several.

"Rose," I said, opening a channel, "this Chief Carter guy... what's he like?"

"From what I hear, Carter is your average, run-of-the-mill cop," Rose replied. "He's an older mage who sports the whole 'gray hair with a matching mustache and beard' look."

"Sounds like someone's grandfather, not a PPD Chief."

"Think five foot eight and a bit saggy in the middle," she answered. "Imagine a short Gandalf, or maybe Santa Claus, and you'll get the idea of it. Nice-enough guy, but he has a tendency of getting edgy when things aren't going smoothly."

"I would imagine an emergency shipment to the Badlands PPD is his idea of things not going smoothly?"

"What do you think, genius?"

"I think this is going to be a tough sell, even if we are PPD."

"You've heard the term straight and narrow?" she asked. "Equal justice for all?"

"Yes."

"He lives to embody them," she said. "He's so rulebook, he makes you look like a dirty gangster dragon. He doesn't even curse."

"What do you mean he doesn't curse?"

"As in no profanity, not his style."

"Sounds like my kind of chief," I said with a nod. *"Do you think he'll give us the weapons?"*

"You're not listening," Rose answered. *"He may sound like your kind of chief, but I can guarantee you we may not be his kind of PPD."*

"What does that mean?"

"Like I've said a billion times now," Rose answered with a sigh, *"no one likes the Badlands PPD."*

"But he will give us the shipment, right?" I asked, knowing that she couldn't possibly know what Chief Carter's thoughts on the subject would be. *"The Directors contacted him through non-official channels."*

"There are several issues," Rose stated. *"His wife is the Req Officer, and she can delay a shipment if the forms aren't to spec,"* Rose answered, *"and they're rarely to spec."*

"Wonderful."

"Then there's the whole 'our PPD is righteous' attitude." She paused and added, *"You do realize we are viewed as monsters outside of the Netherworld?"*

"Yes, but they're in the Netherworld as well."

"We are the PPD in the Badlands, Chief," she answered with a laugh. *"It's not called the 'not so nice' lands or the 'we're not really that good' lands. It's 'Badlands'...for a reason."*

"Yeah, but do they really buy into that?" I asked. *"I mean, we're rough around the edges—"*

"Have you forgotten your first day as chief?" she asked. *"A dead hellion flew through the window, you were shot at, and there were several attempts on your life, some even by criminals."*

The supposition there was that everyone in Netherworld Proper was on the up and up. Obviously that wasn't possible, seeing that there was still a PPD to maintain order. Besides, I'd heard that there was a recent attack on the precinct there and that they were still rebuilding.

Something told me that Rose was just way more cynical than was necessary. To be fair, if I had grown up in the heart of the Badlands, I probably would be, too. The valkyries were hard-asses, sure, but they were always quick to search for solutions to problems, not just to complain that problems existed. Sometimes those solutions were in the form of having a knife stuck in your gut, but they were still solution-focused.

Still, Rose *did* know more about all this than I did.

The fact remained that I was still a neophyte in this world, especially as it related to the politics between the Badlands and Netherworld Proper.

Oh, I knew the history, but historical records have a way of being written in a fashion that makes the historian's side of things look wise and wholesome. After just a few weeks of surviving the harsh realities of the true Badlands, I could only accept about thirty percent of what I'd read regarding our past.

Translation: Netherworld Proper deemed us as monsters.

I groaned.

"Is there a chance we won't come back with weapons?"

"Carter is solid," Rose said, flipping to a more positive outlook. She had a tendency to do that. When I went

negative, she went positive, and vice versa. *"He may be old-school, but he'll do the right thing."*

"And if he doesn't?" I asked. *"I mean the PPD track record hasn't exactly filled me with trust lately."*

"We'll be coming back with weapons, even if I have to start a war, Chief," Rose said in a cold and even voice. *"Even if I have to—"*

"Okay, okay," I said, interrupting her rant. *"Let's hold off on the war for now."* I then moved to change the subject. *"Listen, I had Nimble follow up your lead regarding the Empirics. Can you touch base with him and see if he has any new information on the early delivery or who sent the trigger?"*

She let out a long breath. *"Fine, but we both know it was Scumley."*

"I agree that Bradley *is the most likely candidate,"* I said, using his actual name, *"but we need to know who's bankrolling him. Empirics aren't cheap, and that trigger was state of the art. Bradley can't afford that many Empirics, or a trigger. Someone else is the bank."*

"I'll give you one guess," she said. *"He's the most connected criminal in the Badlands, and his name rhymes with Bake Faster. Any ideas?"*

"Proof, Lieutenant," I demanded, my voice hard. *"We need proof, not hunches."*

"I'll contact the slug and see what he has," Rose answered. A few seconds later, she added, *"I hope you know that if we don't get weapons, we're going to die out here on the Flats."*

"Oh, wow, now I'm all cheered up," I said. *"Maybe we can make you the Chief Morale Officer as well as head badass?"*

"Head Badass is a full-time job, already...so, no thanks." I

could hear the almost-smile in her voice. *"I'll get back to you after I get the info."*

"Thank you, Lieutenant."

"Not like it's a choice, Chief," she replied. *"You'd be lost without me."*

CHAPTER 36

"**We're** closing in on the wall," announced Bernard. "Any sign of hostiles?"

Silk and Butch looked out of their respective windows and shook their heads.

"Can't hide in the Flats," Silk said. "That's the only thing that's good about being out here."

"Oh, I don't know," Butch argued. "The Flatlands have a stark beauty. There's something mesmerizing about the desert."

"How about I drop your mesmerized ass out here without water and see how beautiful you think it is, then?" Silk replied. He grunted. "This place is only good for one thing, leaving it behind. The sooner we get these weapons and back home, the better."

I was with Silk on this one.

The Desolate Flats was exactly that—desolate and featureless. Everywhere I looked there was nothing... except ahead of us.

In the distance, I saw a thin black line on the horizon.

"The wall?" I pointed ahead, and Bernard gave me a short nod. "How large is that thing?"

"Large enough to prevent another war," Bernard answered gruffly. "They put it up to stop us from fighting each other. It's worked well so far."

There had been numerous skirmishes over the years between the two sides, even after the wall was erected, but they were a pittance compared to the Old War. The inability to easily cross into each other's territory was paramount.

But that was common knowledge, even when raised among the valkyries.

What I didn't know was the depth of the safe zones. The Badlands PPD was primarily focused on the main city strip. We didn't play army; we played cops. Neutral infractions between the Badlands and Netherworld Proper was out of our jurisdiction.

"How many neutral areas are there?" I asked.

"Do I look like I work for the Wall Tourism Board?" Bernard barked.

That was an outburst I hadn't expected.

"No," I replied, slowly. "I'd say you look like a cranky, pissed off, old hellion, but I'd still like an answer to my question."

Bernard raised an eyebrow.

Silk and Butch both paused their conversation and looked at me.

"So the dragon has fangs and claws after all," Bernard said with a tight smile. "Thought you were one of the those cerebral dragons who does all his fighting with words. Hope you keep that attitude when they come for us...and they *will* come."

"Neutral areas?" I asked again. "It's important."

"We only need to worry about the one we're headed to...right?"

"Yes and no," I said. "I'd like to know if there is another neutral area we can head to, if we get ambushed."

"Not a bad question," Bernard answered with a nod. "The next neutral area for us is located at the end of our guns."

I still had plenty to learn about the Badlands, but that lesson was clear. Everyone and everything respected superior firepower and force. It was also clear that he wasn't going to answer my actual question.

After cracking open my datapad, I learned that there were a few neutral zones along the border. The problem was there weren't any near here. Even if we did try to make a run for it, we'd run out of fuel before getting halfway.

I let out a slow breath. "What's the plan once we get the weapons?"

"Simple," Bernard answered. "Load up, find a different route through the Flats, so we don't run into the armada of asses trying to take us out, and get you and your crew back to the PPD station."

I picked up motion to our side. The second Deadhaul coming up next to us.

"About time she caught up," Silk said. "You'd better let her get to the wall first, Bernard. They may just shoot us before asking any questions."

"And they won't shoot her?" I asked, trying to see the difference.

"Only if they want today to be their last day," Silk replied as Bernard chuckled. "No one is crazy enough to shoot at her...once they know it's her."

I frowned. "And what is she going to do, just walk up to the wall and flash her badge to let them know she's there?"

"I doubt she'll need the badge," Bernard answered. "Thorny is a force of nature. You don't encounter an earthquake and wonder why the ground is moving."

"No...no you don't," I answered. "You just look for somewhere safe to hide."

"Yep," Bernard said as he waved the second Deadhaul along and fell into line slightly behind them. "I gave up trying to figure her out. I just accept that she is just like the earthquake."

"I think I prefer the earthquake," Silk noted. "At least earthquakes don't shoot at you."

"There is that," Bernard agreed. "She can be a bit twitchy, even for a hellion."

"A bit?" I scoffed. "Her default is shoot first, ask a question, then shoot again."

Butch and Silk nodded.

"I'd like to say she's had a rough life," Bernard said, "but that would just be a lie. Truth is...she's a hellion, and hellions, in case you haven't noticed, are insane."

"I hadn't noticed," I answered, heavy on the snark. "Doesn't everyone enjoy suicide drifting down a cliff, stopping to explode a truck, and then jumping off the side of the cliff to be carried by a dragon to land on another moving truck?"

Bernard chuckled. "Thorny can be a real pisser," he said, pointing. "There's your wall and neutral area. "I'll wait in the truck, if you don't mind."

"Don't want to get out and see the sights of the neutral area?"

"Do you want your weapons?" Bernard said, activating the plexan polarization, essentially making the windows a one-way mirror.

Yes," I said. "We need those weapons."

"Then trust me. You want me to stay in the truck. Chief Carter and I..." He cleared his throat. "Well, let's just say we don't see eye to eye on a few subjects."

"Like?"

"Like what constitutes a crime...nutless," Bernard said, shaking his head. "You think I'm living in dragonville for the view? I've managed to break the law on both sides of this wall."

"You must be pretty popular...in a fleeing criminal sort of way."

"You have no idea," Bernard said, "which is why I'll keep the truck running and remain in the neutral area. Don't want Carter getting any ideas if I step into his jurisdiction."

"Got it," I said as Rose stepped out of her Deadhaul and approached the wall. "I'll let you know when to back it in."

"That's what she said!" Silk yelled as I jumped out of the Deadhaul.

CHAPTER 37

The wall was an imposing structure.

I approached the massive doors that made up the entrance to the neutral area. The wall itself towered over us. They were serious about making this large and strong enough to stop another war. The enormous door was a mix of steel and ironwood. It had to be the largest amount of ironwood in any one place this side of the Badlands.

"How did they get that much ironwood for this door?" I said, marveling at the size of the entrance. "It must have cost a fortune."

"It was donated by the trolls," Rose replied, following my gaze. "It was a gesture of good will at the end of the war, and to prevent future wars."

I looked to either side of the door and noticed the featureless wall had no other openings as far as the eye could see. I also noticed the lack of guns or sentries on this side of the wall.

"No patrols or guns?" I asked. "How do they keep it from being breached?"

Rose pointed behind us.

"Desolate Flats usually ends anyone trying to get here from the Badlands," she said. "Those who make it, won't get past its defenses."

"What defenses?"

Rose picked up a small stone from the ground and hefted it in her hand. She threw it at the wall. It burst into dust on impact.

"Disintegrators," she said with admiration. "Anything that tries to approach gets dusted."

"What about over?" I asked, squinting at the top of the wall. "Someone can just fly over."

"Figured you'd ask that...you being a dragon and all," Rose said, picking up another stone. "Watch."

She flung it over the wall. The stone sailed for about a meter over the wall before bursting into dust like the first.

"Disintegrators?" I asked. "Does the field extend over the wall?"

Rose shook her head. "Wall mounted guns along the interior," she said. "Motion sensitive optics that can see across every spectrum and track. No one is flying over that wall, unless they have a PPD or other authorized vehicle, of course."

"No kidding," I said. "Under?"

"Wall goes down several dozen meters," she answered. "The perimeter is equipped with seismic sensors out to fifty meters. Any digging within that area triggers ground defenses."

"Disintegrators, no doubt?"

Rose nodded. "Like I said, no one gets through that wall without being let in...period."

We approached the large door. Here I noticed turrets mounted on the top of the entrance.

"How is this the entrance to the neutral zone? Doesn't feel very welcoming."

"Where are we standing right now?" Rose asked, looking around.

"Desolate Flats," I said. "The name fits in every respect."

"Which is in the Badlands," she added. "There's a saying, 'nothing good comes out of the Badlands'."

"Which means?"

"Just because it's a neutral zone, doesn't mean anything from this side is welcome *into* the neutral zone."

"I'm beginning to take this animosity toward the Badlands personally," I said, getting angry. "I mean, seriously, what the fuck? It's not like we're actively attacking them. They have their precious wall."

Rose sniffed at my comment as she continued studying the area.

"You know how every family has one crazy uncle or aunt no one really speaks to at the family gatherings?"

"Sure," I said. "The one no one admits to inviting, but calls on when things get dicey and the 'crazy' is needed."

"The Badlands is that family member. They don't want us until they need us...and they never need us." Her eyes stopped on mine. "Nothing good comes out of the Badlands."

"That saying sucks," I said, turning away to examine the door a little more, but not getting too close.

"The saying might suck, but they believed it to the point of putting up this wall."

"I guess. How do we let them know we're here?"

"Like this," Rose said, pulling out her badge and holding it up. "Badlands PPD. We're here to pick up a shipment."

"Hold still for scan," a voice said from the wall. "Scanning in three."

"Don't move," Rose said. "This should do it."

A red beam hit us and traveled the length of our entire bodies.

"Unholy shit!" a voice called out. "If it isn't 'blast a cap in your ass—make your enemies eat glass' Rose Blaze!"

"I see your reputation precedes you," I said under my breath. "Blast a cap in your ass'? Really?"

"I've never made anyone eat glass...at least not that I can recall."

"But you have blasted caps in asses?"

Rose shrugged. "Part of the job, I guess."

"Is that the Badlands new chief?" the voice continued. "Amazing you're still alive, Chief Phoenix."

"Open the damn door, you little Pecker," Rose hissed, resting a hand on one of her guns.

I gave her a look. "I know I'm still a little behind on protocol, but shouldn't you wait to insult him until *after* he opens the door?"

"That's not an insult," Rose answered quietly, and then added loudly, "except maybe to all the small peckers in the *entire* Netherworld!"

"You know, when Chief Carter told me Badlands PPD was visiting, I didn't think they'd send you," Pecker answered. "It must be that cheerful personality that makes you so popular. Oh, wait, that's not it. It's that nasty habit you have of shooting people."

"Pecker?" Rose asked, squeezing enough menace into the word that I wanted to run back to the Deadhaul and leave the wall.

"What?"

"I have an angry caravan of criminals headed this way," she continued. "If they catch up to us because you insist on fucking around at the door, I will come back, I will find you, and I will use my particular set of skills to hurt you."

The door slid open.

A goblin with a narrow, gray face that was littered with wrinkles and creases peeked around the edge. His ears were long and pointed, and they had hair poking out of their holes. He wiped his nose on his dirty lab coat as he motioned for us to come closer.

"Did you disable the synaptic scramblers?" Rose asked, staring at him hard. "I'd like to know *before* one of us tries to use connectors?"

"Synaptic scramblers?" I asked. "What the hell is that?"

"They jam and disable all connector signals," Rose answered. "You try to use your connector when they're active, and they fry you into unconsciousness."

"And if disabled?" I asked.

"They prevent connector signals when disabled."

I looked around. "Where are they?"

"Just inside the neutral zone," Rose replied. "They're designed to take out anything fierce enough to get past the wall. He likes to leave them on…just in case."

"Oh, yeah...*those* scramblers," Pecker said, snapping his fingers with an evil smile. "Keep forgetting to disable those things. Silly me."

"I'm glad I could remind you," Rose said, resting a hand on her gun. "Next time, I'll just use my guns to jog your memory."

"Why so serious, Rose?" Pecker answered with a chuckle as four armed guards holding some kind of shotgun-Gatling hybrid appeared next to him in the doorway. "You really need to loosen up, which I'd be more than happy to assist you with."

"Before or after I lobotomize you?"

"Sheesh, these bitchy hellions...always ready to shoot someone or something."

"Who is he, again?" I asked. "Even better, why is he here?"

"Think about what Nimble does for the Badlands PPD, just less slime."

"Good old Nimble," Pecker said. "How is the old slug these days? Tell him I said 'Fuck you' for that last package he sent me."

"I'll make sure to relay the message," Rose affirmed. "Is Chief Cart—?"

"Welcome to the neutral zone," Carter interrupted, stepping out from behind the guards. He did resemble a short Gandalf —Santa Claus hybrid. "Good to see you made it in one piece." He studied the area behind us for a moment. "Are you one truck light? I was told three."

"We had some company on Deadman's Drift," Rose grunted. "Had to lose one of the trucks."

"Deadman's Drift?" Carter said, staring hard at Rose

and then the mirrored Deadhaul windshield. "I see. Was that your idea?"

Rose stared back, unflinching. "Yes. I didn't think we'd have company, though."

"You'd be surprised who comes out of the woodwork when you're vulnerable and exposed," Carter egged her on.

Rose nodded.

"I'm Chief Phoenix," I said, holding out my hand. "It's a pleasure to meet my counterpart on the Netherworld Proper side."

"Chief," Carter said, taking my hand. "Rumor has it that you're a decent fellow. You consider honor a commodity."

"Shouldn't everyone?" I questioned.

Carter let go of my hand and ran his fingers through his beard. "I'd say it's paramount. I'm just not used to seeing it from the head of the Badlands PPD."

I couldn't blame him for feeling that way.

"Wish we could be meeting under better circumstances," he sighed, "but you know how it is with the PPD, 'Protect, Provide, and Defend'."

I glanced at Rose, who deliberately ignored me.

"I was told it was 'Punish, Pulverize, and Destroy'," I said, glancing Rose's way again. "I'll have to update my terminology."

"There are likely even more colorful definitions for our acronym," he chuckled.

"Indeed," I agreed. "Did our Directors contact you?"

Carter nodded. "I believe we have some weapons for you. Let's get to work. You don't have much time. If you signal your trucks, I'll have my men help you with the loading."

"I really appreciate it," I said as Rose turned and swung an arm to the Deadhauls, motioning for them to back in. "We'll be out of your way as soon as possible."

CHAPTER 38

*A*s the trucks backed into place, a few machines carrying boxes of weaponry appeared.

"Did you find out how it happened?" Carter asked.

"Still digging into it."

"Blowing up a PPD station is a serious offense. I assume you plan on apprehending those responsible?"

My assumption was that he guessed we'd just kill those involved. Nothing good comes from the Badlands, right?

"I do," I said, my voice hard. "Once we secure these weapons, and restore our personnel, we'll handle it— that's our priority."

"You can't let an attack on the PPD go unanswered. The law must be upheld."

"I agree," I said as the Deadhauls backed into the neutral area. "I'll make sure to prosecute those responsible to the fullest extent of the law."

"That's something I'd like to see," Carter said. "The law being upheld in the Badlands."

Carter's men, along with Butch, Doe, Graffon, and a supervising Silk started loading the Deadhauls.

"I'm the same way, and we *will* find those responsible and apprehend them."

"You'll have to excuse me," Chief Carter said, "but the Badlands isn't exactly known for its law-abiding population...or police force."

It was a subtle jab at the Badlands PPD that I chose to ignore. I wasn't going to get into it with the Chief who was providing us with weapons to protect ourselves. That didn't mean I was going to let him insult us, though.

"Maybe in the past, with other chiefs," I said. "But under my guidance and with the assistance of my team, the Badlands PPD will uphold the law and honor the badge."

Carter moved over to one side as the rest of the crew kept loading.

"I want to apologize for that, but I needed to know where your head was at...you being a dragon and all," he said, "You don't have the best of reputations."

"I understand," I said, and I did. "I still have some difficulty convincing my own people a dragon can be a PPD chief."

Carter nodded as he watched the weapons being loaded.

"Each truck will have the same load-out, just in case you lose another," Carter said. "I reckon the reports of the explosion on Deadman's Drift was your group?"

"That was us, or rather my second-in-command," I answered. "We had a Hellion Sweeper on our"—I remembered what Rose had said about the cursing—"tail ready to shove us off the mountain."

"That's one way of dealing with it," Carter said with a nod.

We stopped talking for a few minutes, opting instead to just watch the trucks get loaded. It was definitely going to be a tighter fit riding back than it was getting here. Being down one truck didn't help, either.

One thing was for certain, though. I wasn't going to be sitting on anyone's lap.

"I apologize for putting you out like this," I said, finally. "I realize we weren't due a shipment until next month."

He waved my words away.

"The head of supplies is going to grumble at me something fierce, but she'll eventually come around."

"A real ball breaker, eh?"

"Watch your tongue, son," he said with a stern look. "That's my wife you're talking about."

"Oh…shi…shoot," I rasped. "I apologize, Chief. I didn't know."

There was a hint of a grin on his lips. "No way you could have."

"Right," I said. "Mind if I ask you a question related to the PPD?"

"By all means, go ahead."

I took a deep breath. "I think I may have more criminal elements than officers in my force."

His face grew stern, making it clear that he and I were two birds of a feather. You don't wear the badge if you're not on the up and up. Sure, there were different levels of 'good' in the world, especially when it came to the

Badlands, but an officer should never disrespect the badge.

"Let me give you a piece of advice," Carter said. "Chief to chief."

"Trust no one?"

"Sure," he mused, "that could be one way to deal with it —if you want to live with a gun in your hand every moment, looking over your shoulder constantly."

He had just described life in the Badlands.

"You have another method?"

He nodded. "Make your people respect you more than they fear the criminals. Add a splash of fear of your own. Shouldn't be too hard, you being a dragon and all."

"I don't want my people scared of me."

"Can't be helped," Carter said. "Reflex with dragons... and chiefs."

"Okay, but if I do that...how do I get past that fear when I need to?"

"Show them you care, and they'll brave the nine levels of hell with you."

"Chief?"

Carter and I both turned.

He chuckled.

"I think its for you," Carter said when he saw Silk. "I'll go make sure the manifest is correct and light a fire under my team."

"What is it?" I asked as Carter headed over to the loading bay.

"You remember when Bernard said we had about a day before they caught up with us?"

"Yes?" I said, a knot forming in my gut. "Are you saying he was off on his calculations?"

Silk flew up a few meters and then pointed. I followed his arm with my gaze. My eyesight was highly developed and I caught the plume of dust after a few seconds.

"Dust storm? Tell me that's a dust storm."

"In your dreams. Those bas"—he looked around to check where Chief Carter was— "those bastards are the ones from the cliff."

"Fuck me," I said, mostly to myself. "We need to go."

CHAPTER 39

"We almost done?" I asked, heading to the rear of the Deadhauls.

Rose looked up at my words, or rather the tone. Apparently, hellions had a very sensitive ear to tonal stress in voices and right now, I was stressed.

"What's going on, Chief?" Rose asked, looking out into the horizon.

I remembered we couldn't use our connectors due to the jamming.

"Seems like our mutual friend was off with his estimate," I answered her. "We have, judging from the distance, about an hour…maybe two before they show up."

"Before who shows up?" Pecker said, popping his head in between us.

"What the fu—"

"Eh eh eh," Pecker said, wagging a finger at me. "Language. Chief likes to run a profanity-free zone."

I was glad I caught myself as Pear grabbed on to my leg.

"ZeeZee!" he yelled. "Can we go boom again?"

"Well, dip me in honey and spank my bum until it's done," Pecker said. "Is that a bragon?"

"Yes," I said, and then, mostly out of reflex, added, "No, you can't examine or experiment on him."

"The slug asked, didn't he?" Pecker said, looking disappointed. "It won't be *too* invasive. Just a few incisions here and there. So hard to find a live one."

"Do you know Hilda?" I asked.

"Of the Dragon's Teeth valkyries?"

"Is there another?"

"No, thankfully," Pecker said with a sigh. "One of her is enough for the entire Netherworld."

"She's his mom," I said in a slow voice, letting it sink in thoroughly. "So, technically, while I *can* let you examine him, you really don't want to. If you do, I can promise you she *will* be invasive, with a few incisions here and there. I'm sure you won't miss your arms or legs."

"On second thought," Pecker replied, quickly, "I think one of the journals from about a hundred years ago discussed bragon anatomy at length. No need for me to *personally* examine him."

I stared at him. "So, you'll just read the article?"

"I'll just read the article," Pecker said, stepping away from Pear and moving closer to Rose. "So, Rose, whats going on?"

"Our violent escort is closer than we calculated," Rose said. "About two hours out."

"You can see that far?"

"I can't," Rose said, pointing at me. "He can."

"Dragons are fascinating," Pecker answered.

"Are we almost loaded up?" I asked.

"Twenty minutes and we should be done," Doe replied. "Do you think we can take some of these rocket launchers?"

"Do we have room?"

"I'll make room."

"One each truck," I confirmed, worried that Doe actually almost sounded happy. "No more."

"You can't go back over the Flats," Pecker noted. "They'll intercept you and that's all she wrote. Even with the weapons, there's only a handful of you against"—he pulled out a pair of high-powered binoculars—"at least a few hundred. Even with the hellions, a dragon, an immature bragon, a faceless, a demonoid, a dark fae, and a malkyrie, you won't last more than a few minutes."

"Hellions?" I asked.

"I'm a goblin, Chief, but I'm not stupid," Pecker laughed. "You took Deadman's Drift. Only two hellions are crazy enough to take that pass, and one of them is standing next to me."

If he knew that Bernard was with us, it was very likely that Chief Carter knew as well. That he didn't have that fact checked was a testament to his own honor. Obviously, Bernard had aided the Badlands Paranormal Police Department in its time of need. That must have carried some weight with Carter.

It would have with me.

"What about all the vehicles after us?" I asked.

"You'll find that many of those now in the group took

a longer route," Pecker answered. "The ones who followed you down, probably doubled back up the cliff. How this group got here so fast is another story. It's almost as if they knew you were headed this way."

Rose and I looked at each other.

"Well, duh," said Rose, giving Pecker a look. "Where else would we be heading?"

"No, I mean…" The goblin coughed. "Never mind."

"We still have to get back, though," Rose sighed. "All right, Pecker, what do you suggest?"

"There's a pass through the Dragon's Teeth—Goblin's Gauntlet."

Rose stared at him for a second. I'd seen that look before. It was her 'I'm going to shoot you now' look.

"You're trying to kill us."

"No," Pecker answered, putting his hands up. "*They're* trying to kill you. I just gave you the only way out. Once we give you the weapons, you're on your own. We lock up and leave you to your fate."

Pecker looked out of the door at the Desolate Flats.

"Your team won't even offer support?" I asked.

"We just did," Pecker argued. "You have two Deadhauls full of weapons. As far as last stands go, it's not a bad place to die. If you park the trucks just so, you can use them as barriers. You may even last a few extra minutes."

"We are not dying here," Rose said, her voice steel. "I didn't come this far to come this far."

"That's the spirit," Pecker answered. "From here, Goblin's Gauntlet is due east." He pointed. "When you see Heaven's Fang, you hang a right. Can't miss it." He smiled almost proudly. "The first drop off is called Pucker Factor Twenty."

That caused me to jolt. "What kind of name is that?"

"The appropriate kind," Pecker answered. "You'll see." He then shook my hand. "Good luck out there. If I don't hear from you I'll assume you didn't make it, in which case this is good bye."

"Fuck off, Pecker." Rose said.

"Love you too, Rose," Pecker said and walked off into the neutral zone.

"I'd prefer you kept the use of that language to a minimum around me, young lady," Chief Carter stated as he snuck up behind us.

"Oh," Rose replied, standing up straight. "I'm sorry, sir. I didn't know you were there."

I blinked rapidly at her.

What. The. Fuck?

So, a hellion can calm a bragon, and a Chief Carter can calm a hellion?

Obviously, his little piece of sage advice about instilling a hint of fear in people was damn solid.

"You'll do fine, Chief Phoenix," Carter said, holding out his hand again. I shook it. "Follow Pecker's advice and let your hellions take the wheel on both vehicles."

The look in his eyes told me he damn well knew who was in the second Deadhaul.

"Thank you, Chief Carter," I replied, giving him a short nod. "We'll do just that."

"Rose," he said, patting her shoulder, "you take care of yourself, do you hear me?"

"Yes, sir."

Seriously. I mean...come on!

"Good," Carter said, before heading back to the doors. "Until next time, then."

"Until next time," I called after him, fascinated at whatever type of magic he was using to cow Rose. "Until next time, indeed."

CHAPTER 40

"We need to rearrange the teams," I said.

"Tell me about it," Rose said, walking to her Deadhaul. "If we're doing Goblin's Gauntlet, I'm driving."

I opened up a group channel.

"New teams," I said. *"Rose, Graffon, Pear, and me are in Alpha One. Bernard, Silk, Butch and Doe in Alpha Two."*

Rose was on her phone relaying the information to Bernard.

"Goblin's Gauntlet!" Bernard's voice carried over to our Deadhaul. "Are you insane?"

"Is it that bad?" I asked as Rose held the phone away from her ear. "He seems pretty upset."

"Not really," she answered. "I expected him to try and shoot me. This is much calmer than I thought he would react."

I looked over at the second Deadhaul. It was rocking from Bernard's movement. Whatever he was doing in there, he was angry.

"Tell him not to break the vehicle," I said. "We still need to get home."

She ended the call.

"Let's give the pissed off hellion sitting in a truck full of weapons some time before I relay your message," Rose suggested. "Wouldn't want him to vent all that anger our way."

"Good point," I said. "Has he ever done this Goblin's Gauntlet?"

"That's probably the real reason he's upset," Rose said with a malicious smile. "He's never run it successfully, and I have…twice."

"Which means?" I asked, not understanding this hellion dynamic. "You have to teach him?"

"I have to run point, and he has to follow *my* lead."

"So," I said slowly, "this is some kind of pissing contest?"

"When we last faced the Gauntlet, I was learning," she explained. "By completing it more than once, he has to call me master."

I was about to cue in the evil laugh.

"Honestly, I don't care which one of you needs to lead," I said, opting to ignore hellion plays of dominance. "Just be straight with me here, okay? How dangerous is this Goblin's Gauntlet?"

"Remember Deadman's Drift?"

"Like I could forget our near fatal leap," I snapped back, upset. "Of course, I remember the Drift."

"The Gauntlet will make that look like a pleasant afternoon drive," she said. "Only the most insane hellions have taken the Gauntlet more than once and completed it. Bernard is probably shitting his pants right now."

"Because he has to follow you?"

"Because he's probably going to die," Rose answered her voice serious. "You may want to move Silk, Butch, and Doe to our Deadhaul."

"We don't have the room."

"We do if we relocate some of the weapons to Alpha Two."

The look on her face was stern. She wasn't just using bravado here. This wasn't Rose puffing out her chest.

"You're serious?" I asked.

"Pucker Factor Twenty is a sixty degree slope, leading into a drift turn, and followed by a sheer cliff road barely wide enough for a vehicle half the width of a Deadhaul."

"Oh, okay," I said, nodding frantically. "So you're basically saying that we're all going to die."

"It gets worse," she continued. "I won't share because then you'd try and climb down on your own. Don't do that, Chief. I can guarantee it *would* kill you."

"Great, so we *are* going to die."

"Not with me behind the wheel, we aren't." She opened the group channel. *"Silk, Butch, and Doe, when I pull up next to you, find room in Alpha One, even if that means moving weapons to Alpha Two."*

"What?" Silk said. *"I was just getting comfortable. Now we have to move?"*

"Only if you want to live," Rose answered. *"Bernard has never completed the Gauntlet. You can stay there if you like, of course."*

"What? Fuck no!" Silk yelled and darted out of Alpha

Two when it came to a stop a few meters from us. *"I'd like to actually make it through this trip, thank you."*

"Butch, Doe, and Graffon," Rose instructed. *"Relocate some of our weapons to Alpha Two to make room for the entire team."*

"Don't touch the rocket launchers," Doe said. *"We always have room for rocket launchers."*

"This has to be a joke," I said.

"How often have you heard me joke?" Rose asked, stepping out of the Deadhaul. "I'll explain it to Bernard. He's a hellion. He'll see my point. I know I would."

"That you have such little faith in his driving"—I looked over at Alpha Two—"the hellion who taught you, that you're not willing to trust the crew to him and his driving ability?"

She raised an eyebrow at me for a second before turning toward Bernard's truck.

"See? You're not even a hellion and you see my point," she said, walking away. "You may want to help unload some weapons. More hands working means the faster we get on our way."

"How in the nine levels can this get worse?" I asked, jumping out of Alpha One.

It wasn't even twenty seconds later that I heard voices rising from the second Deadhaul.

"You want me to what?" Bernard yelled, stepping out of the vehicle and slamming the door. "You must have baked your hellion mind, Thorny. Fuck that, and fuck you!"

I looked over and saw Bernard walk towards the wall. He was heading right toward the neutral area entrance.

Rose walked back to our Deadhaul, shaking her head.

"I really thought he'd be okay with it," Rose said, surprise entering her voice. "He refused to drive second to me as a junior, except that's exactly what he is on the Gauntlet."

"That may be true, but he doesn't see it that way."

"Obviously, since he's walking to the neutral zone," Rose retorted, then spoke on the group channel. *"Dark Succubus, you're up!"*

"Roger, Bloody Rose," Graffon answered. *"Can I have Doe for my co-pilot. He's a good buddy."*

"Call me a 'good buddy' again," Doe started, *"and I'll shoot you, Lieutenant Rose-style."*

"Doe, go assist"—a brief pause and a short cough—*"Dark Succubus."*

"Roger that, Bloody Rose!" Graffon replied. *"I'm locked and loaded and ready to roll! Let's do this!"*

"What have I created?" Rose groaned, rubbing a hand down her face. *"This is going to end badly."*

CHAPTER 41

"*I*s he really not going to drive?" I looked at the receding figure of Bernard. "What did you say to piss him off that much?"

"Nothing," Rose answered. "I gave him a way to walk away and save face without having to admit his driving ability was inferior to mine. He's actually very grateful."

"I never thought to see it that way," I said.

"Why would you? You're not a hellion."

I wanted to say "Thankfully," but didn't want to rock the cart even further. While I didn't have a lot of memories in regards to how dragons treated each other —*competed* with each other—I assumed that it wasn't much different to hellions. We were both stubborn races.

"Do you think Graf—Dark Succubus can handle the Gauntlet?"

"I don't know," she admitted, "but if there is anyone among Alpha besides me who can, it's her."

Graffon started the engine of her Deadhaul with a roar.

"Let's put some space between us and this wall," Rose said, starting her engine as well. "Once they realize where we're going, we'll lose half of the pursuit."

"Sounds good."

"No, not good," Rose shot back. "The crazy bastards who do follow us will be the ones we need to dispatch while trying not to die."

"Right," I said, shaking myself back to the realities of our situation. "This *is* bad."

"Focus, Chief," Rose said grinning. "I don't plan on dying today. This may be bad, but we're worse."

"Nothing good comes out of the Badlands," I droned with a nod.

I wanted to grin, but I still had problems with that sentiment, so what came out was kind of a sneer-grin thing.

It didn't seem to matter to Rose.

"Fucking right," she said. "Let's show these fuckers what real driving looks like."

"Fuckersfuckersfuckers!"

Rose let Pear have that one.

"*Dark Succubus*," Rose commanded through the connector, "*Ride my ass and don't let up.*"

"*Copy that, Bloody Rose,*" she replied.

"I'd be happy to do that at some point, too, Rose," Silk snarked from the backseat.

"You'd die trying."

"Worth it."

I had the feeling that Silk's comment would have ended in a meeting with Human Resources at any other PPD in the world.

Rose's grin only deepened, though.

Did she have a thing for Fae? No way.

"Humpyhumpyhumpy," Pear sang softly, shocking me that he even knew what they were talking about.

We sped off heading east.

Even though the trucks were weighed down with weapons, we were making good time. I looked out of the window, and the plume of dust had gotten closer. I focused my vision and saw the assortment of vehicles veering slightly in our direction.

"How are they—?"

"Same way you're seeing them," Rose answered before I could finish. "We're kicking up a dust trail."

"Shit."

"Before you ask," she added, "there's no way to hide our dust plume."

"How soon to the Gauntlet?" I asked.

"Soon," Rose said. "Strap your asses in back there. I don't care if you have to sit on someone's lap, people, get secure!"

"There's no room back here!" Silk yelled to the front. "We're close, but we're not *that* close."

"Sit on someone's lap, if you have to," Rose yelled back. "Either that, or I'll open a door and you can walk home… and I'm not slowing down as you make your exit—just to be clear."

"You can sit on my lap," Butch offered.

"Screw you, Butch!"

"Don't tempt me."

Rose turned the truck left and right a few times, causing Silk to bounce around in the back.

"Eeek," Silk yelped. "Fine, I'll sit on Butch's lap."

"Turning out to be a good day, after all," Butch said as the buckles unlatched and re-latched.

"Gross," Silk grumbled. "I'd better not feel anything growing down there, Butch. If I do, I swear I'll punch you in the neck."

"I'll give you a safe word."

There was a moment of silence. Then, Silk said, "Open a door, I've decided to jump!"

"Too late," answered Rose. "Enjoy your 'ride'."

Yep, this would definitely be a meeting with Human Resources at any other precinct in the world.

"What's your damage today, anyway?" Silk grumped.

"You mean besides Rose pissing off her teacher to the point where he left us right before attempting another suicide run while being chased by psycho criminals out to kill us?"

"Well…when you put it like that…"

"Yeah," I said. "I wouldn't aggravate her anymore right now." I glanced at Butch. "Or him."

Rose white-knuckled the steering wheel and pushed the Deadhaul faster.

"I'm going to need you to activate the solar and electric power plants right before we hit Pucker Factor Twenty," Rose said coolly, flexing her jaw muscles.

"While you have the engine running?" I asked. "Didn't Francis say the engine couldn't take that much force?"

"We don't have a choice, we need to hit that first drop at speed and use the momentum to get us through the drift and over the first straightaway."

"Wouldn't it be better to take it slow?"

"I'm sorry," she shot back, "how many times have you completed this run, again?"

"Zero times," I mumbled.

"Exactly. Zero times. Here's an idea, how about we leave the calculations to those of us that have actually driven the Gauntlet and survived?"

"Point taken," I said. "Just making an observation."

"Only observation I want from you on this run is how close those bastards are to our asses. Think you can handle that?"

"I'm on it," I said. "Are we close to the Gauntlet?"

Rose nodded and motioned forward with her chin. In the distance, like an enormous middle finger, Heaven's Fang jutted into the sky.

Pecker's words came back to me: *"When you see Heaven's Fang, you hang a right. Can't miss it."*

Rose pulled the wheel hard to the right. Not hard enough to cause a drift, but enough to change our course...toward the caravan of death following us.

"You better pull those straps harder, Chief," Rose said, tightening her own harness. "Entrance is coming up fast, and we're going to need that boost to beat these assholes into the Gauntlet."

Now I understood why she wanted the solar and electric power plants ready to go. We were no longer being chased, but racing perpendicular to the armada of vehicles on an intercept course with us.

"Think we'll make it?" I asked, seeing a rocky outcropping that I could only imagine was the entrance to the Gauntlet.

"When I tell you," Rose pointed to the dashboard

switches, "solar first, then electric. Got it?"

"Got it—solar, then electric."

"Dark Succubus," Rose called over the group channel, *"follow my lead. Fifty meters from the entrance to the Gauntlet, you activate all the power plants for exactly ten seconds. Solar, then electric. Copy?"*

"Copy, Bloody Rose," Graffon answered. *"Fifty meters to entrance, solar then electric power plants for ten seconds."*

"It's going to launch your fat ass Deadhaul for several meters," Rose continued. *"Ride the road, gravity is your friend here. Accelerate into the first drift early and pull out fast.*

"That's what she said," Silk said with a chuckle.

"Shut it, fae," Rose said. *"Copy, Dark Succubus?"*

"Copy, Bloody Rose," Graffon responded. *"I have the need....the need for speed!"*

Rose glanced at me as if to say "what have I done?" and then focused on the road ahead again.

"Chief," she said, "use those super eyeballs of yours and tell me how close they are. Also, tell me their lead vehicles. This is going to be tight, but we can squeeze it in."

"That's what she—" Silk started.

"I *will* shoot you," Rose said her voice steel. "I told you to shut it and I meant it."

Silk shut it.

"Am I looking for anything in particular?" I asked, peering out of my window.

"Sweepers," Rose said. "I need to know how many."

I focused my vision and saw the armada arcing closer to us. The rear of the armada was made up of slower vehicles. Heavy trucks and troop transport types. The middle section had smaller vehicles, mid-sized trucks and cars. The front of the armada was made up of more sleek supercars and surprisingly, Sweepers.

"I count three Sweepers," I said, amazed at their velocity. They were easily keeping pace with the supercars. "How are they going that fast?"

"Hellion tech is superior," Rose said. "On my mark, remember solar then electric."

"Solar, then electric."

The entrance to the Gauntlet raced up at us. When we were almost at the edge, Rose yelled.

"Now!"

I hit the solar power plant switch followed by the electric. The Deadhaul lurched forward, screaming as we picked up even more speed. We hit the entrance of the Gauntlet and soared into the air. Behind us I could hear Graffon's Deadhaul do the same as she hit the power plants.

I looked down and regretted it instantly.

CHAPTER 42

"*R*ose?" I said warily. "Where…the fuck…is the road?"

I looked out the window and realized the sixty degree slope looked closer to ninety degrees when you're racing over the edge and across what looked like a bottomless chasm.

"Pucker Factor Twenty," Rose said with a sick grin. "You thought I was kidding? Pucker up, its going to be a rough landing."

"You never said anything about a bottomless chasm," I said, looking into the darkness below us. "What the hell, Rose?"

"That's probably where it leads," Rose said. "Brace for impact."

The Deadhaul hung in the air for what seemed an eternity, but was probably closer to five seconds. Five seconds airborne with a truck full of weapons and no apparent landing gives a new definition to Pucker Factor Twenty. If we survived this, I doubted I could use a bathroom ever again. Parts of my body clamped up so tightly, that they would never open without surgery.

We landed across the chasm with a bone-jarring crash, and Rose immediately pulled the wheel a hard right. The Deadhaul's fat ass swerved as we slid into a drift. The next second we were racing out of it to approach a narrow road...one that looked too narrow for a Deadhaul. Right before the entrance of the road, on one side, sat a fairly tall mound of dirt. As we got closer I realized what it was.

It wasn't a mound, it was a ramp.

"Are you fucking kidding me?" I said, raising my voice. "No way, Rose...no way!"

I gripped the metal handle near my door and held on tight enough to leave a depression in the material.

Rose angled the Deadhaul, so that one set of tires raced over the ramp. We rolled up the ramp on one side and Rose placed a boot in the center of the dashboard for balance as we tilted sideways and raced down the narrow road with one set of tires on the road and the other on the wall adjacent to the road.

"Rinse and repeat, Dark Succubus," Rose commanded. I saw the sweat on her face and realized she was as scared as I looked. *Do what I do, or you don't make it back. Copy.*

"Co...copy, Bloody Rose," Graffon answered. *"On two wheels? Really?"*

Behind us, I could hear the crashes of the vehicles that undershot the first drop and sailed into the chasm walls. A thunderous crunch notified us that Graffon had landed. We were on the other side of the narrow road as Graffon approached.

We headed toward a small circular area that led to another wider road.

"You got this," Rose said, activating the rear exterior camera with a flick of a switch. She then started to turn the Deadhaul around. *"Next part is going to be tricky, make sure you back in and use your rear camera. I'll circle around, get you in place."*

"Back in?" I asked. "Why would she need to back in?"

"Keep an eye out for hostiles, Chief," Rose said, accelerating forwards with the Deadhaul facing backwards. "They're going to start shooting."

"Who's going to start shooting?" I asked. "I don't see—?"

Graffon had entered the circular area as Rose executed another circuit around the circle getting the other Deadhaul behind us.

Both trucks were facing backwards.

"Listen carefully Dark Succubus," Rose said. *"Under the steering column and to the right is the rocket switch. If you go left of the column you activate the self-destruct...do not activate the self-destruct. Copy?"*

"Copy," Graffon answered. *"Is there a reason we're backing into this part of the Gauntlet?"*

"You're going to find out in about five seconds," Rose answered. *"Once you back into the next part and feel your Deadhaul leaning, activate the rockets. They take a few seconds to engage. Make sure your rear camera is on. Copy?"*

"Copy."

"Rose?" I said as we backed into the road. "Why are we facing backwards?"

"Get your guns out, Chief," Rose said. "This next part

is called the Mobius strip. If we go in facing forward, we'll end up backwards on the landing."

I gulped.

"Did you say landing?"

"Some of these fuckers *are* going to make it," she continued, pointing at the oncoming rush of bad guys, "but they'll be facing the wrong way. That's where you come in. Blast them as they arrive, and we'll thin the herd even more."

I heard Graffon's rockets fire and they disappeared.

CHAPTER 43

A mobius strip is a surface with only one side and only one boundary. It's un-orientable, meaning that once you are on one, you're as lost as fuck, not knowing which way is up or down, and you're basically screwed sideways.

This part of the Gauntlet consisted of three nested loops.

Rose leaned forward as the rear of our Deadhaul tipped down, and activated the rockets. The roar of the engine was dwarfed by the blast of the rockets as I realized they were keeping us attached to the strip by adding a constant speed and exerting consistent inward force.

"Fuck me!" I said as we fell backward. "Rose, a little warning would've been nice."

"Fuckmefuckmefuckme...weee!"

"No way to explain this part," Rose yelled as the Deadhaul vibrated and shook its way down the strip.

"Except...to go...through it. Out...of...everyone here... you'll be the least...affected. Get...ready!"

Rather than launch us off the strip, the rockets kept us attached to the surface. We blasted backward and downward, took the first loop and rotated sideways into the next loop, which turned us forward and upward into the last loop, which turned us sideways again and righted our position.

Groans from the back of the cargo area filled the Deadhaul.

I felt unaffected because the Mobius Strip had just taken us through a basic dragon flight maneuver. Dragons have an internal compass that compensates for aerial disruption and acrobatics. Simply put, no matter what we do in the air...we don't get dizzy or disoriented.

After the last loop, we shot out into space. I saw Graffon's Deadhaul land ahead of us and take off, rockets still firing. We landed a few seconds later on a wide road, which immediately made me nervous because it was so ordinary.

"What the fuck, Rose?" Silk moaned. "You couldn't have given us a heads up you were going to try and make us revisit breakfast?"

"That was the best lap dance I've ever had," said a serene sounding Butch.

"Ah...gross, man!"

Pear was clapping his hands gleefully.

"Againagainagainagain again!" he yelled. "Zeezee, again!"

At least someone was enjoying themselves...besides Butch.

"We're not done yet," Rose said, swerving around a crater that formed two seconds earlier in front of us. "Stay strapped in. This is going to get swervy."

"Bloody Rose, this is Dark Succubus, copy," Graffon called out. *"Been managing to avoid the craters, but it's getting dicey."*

"I read you," Rose answered. *"This section is the Mirage. Look for the shimmering air, it appears right where the next crater is going to form. You have about two to three seconds warning. Stay alert. We have a few miles of this, and then we'll be out of the Gauntlet."*

Behind us, as Rose predicted, I heard vehicles land on the road.

"How the fuck did they make it through that madness?"

"Doesn't matter," Rose said. "Time to introduce them to the error of their ways, Chief."

I made my way to the rear gun port, climbing over boxes as best I could. It reminded me of the tunnel dives Hilda used to put me through during training. No room, dark, jutting edges, and a heaping dose of claustrophobia. At least there weren't any snakes here.

Rose had hit the brakes, swerved, and then floored it again.

I knew this because it threw me around and dumped me head-first into the small section of space that had no boxes.

It took a little doing, but I oriented myself and stuck my wings out just enough to grant me some measure of stability.

Next, I repositioned the mini-gun, and opened fire. The lead car, a sleek black Hurricane similar to Rose's

PPD vehicle, didn't stand a chance. The rounds sliced through the hood, windshield, and engine like a giant scythe, cutting the car in two before it exploded.

"Fuck yeah!" Silk screamed, obviously looking at the little screen that showed the rear camera view. "Show them, Chief!"

"I can't see anything," Butch complained.

"You got your lap dance," Silk shot back. "Deal with it."

"Oooh," cooed Butch. "I like your tone."

"Gross!"

The next vehicle wasn't going to be as easy.

It was a Hellion Sweeper.

Graffon's Deadhaul swung up next to us.

"Rose, we have a Sweeper back here!" I yelled, opening fire. The rounds just bounced off its armored exterior. "We need something with a little more punch than this mini-gun."

I'd thought to use Pinky, but there was no easy way to do that, without opening the doors, and...no.

"Rockets!" Doe said over the connector. "It's rocket time!

I could almost hear his grin.

Glancing through the window for a quick peek at Graffon's truck, I saw something really strange on Doe's face. In the short time I had been in the Badlands PPD, nothing and no one had elicited a genuine smile from the faceless. Until now.

Doe undid his harness and started crawling out of the window, making his way to the top of the Deadhaul. I was going to yell at him, but what would have been the point?

"Where are the rockets?" I asked.

Butch reached back, slamming his hand on one of the containers.

"Why are there three of those?" I asked. "I expressly said one per truck."

"Chief," Doe said, *"you can never have too many rockets or rocket launchers."*

"Rockets?" Rose yelled back at us. "Don't you dare fire those things in here! You'll set off every combustible weapon in the cargo hold."

"How do you expect us to fire them then?" I yelled back.

"Get your asses *on* the Deadhaul and fire from there," Rose shot back.

That explained why Doe had climbed to the roof.

"Any suggestions on *how* I'm supposed to get up on the roof, Rose?" I yelled back at her, my ire on the rise.

"I don't care how you do it, Chief," she argued back. "Just stop those Sweepers. Now!"

"Son of a bitch," I hissed as I made my way back through the mess of boxes to the front. "One of you has to get back there and take over for me."

"Don't have to ask me twice," Silk announced, unbuckling the harness.

There wasn't really much room to leap off Butch's lap, but Silk had somehow managed it.

"Nope," Butch said, grabbing the dark fae by the shoulder. He got up and stuck Silk in the chair. "You stay there, puddin' cup. I'll take care of this."

"Puddin' cup?" Silk choked. "Dude…ew."

Butch started the climb back as I headed for the passenger window.

"Lay down suppressing fire until I get on the roof, then lock her up tight," I called out, pressing Whoosh and forming my scales. *"Ready, Doe?"*

"Locked and loaded, Chief!" Doe yelled. *"Let's do this!"*

Graffon had moved her truck close to ours. A thud confirmed that Doe had jumped onto the top of Rose's Deadhaul.

"I'm on your roof, Chief," Doe confirmed. *"Come on up and let's end these bastards."*

It was becoming clear that this road trip was turning Alpha Team especially rambunctious. I tried to remember what Hilda called it when we behaved this way.

It suddenly came to me as I got ready to pull myself up to the roof.

"Ok, Doe! Let's go full Rambo on these fuckers! Butch, open it up!"

Butch kicked open the backdoor, with a mini-gun in each hand, and opened fire on the vehicles behind us.

Doe jumped forward and opened fire with his guns.

I was behind him a second later. Gunfire erupted from the vehicles. The Sweeper accelerated and tried to crush us.

Graffon pulled ahead and away from us.

"Go go go!" Doe yelled as I climbed up and rolled onto the roof of the Deadhaul a second before the Sweeper slammed into us. *"Shit!"*

Doe rolled to the side from the impact. I jumped forward, grabbing his leg as he nearly slid off the Deadhaul.

"This is the only ride we have," I yelled out loud, pulling him back. "Try to stay on it."

"Roger, Chief!"

He extended the sight on his rocket launcher and plunged a rocket down the tube.

"What are you waiting for?" I said with a grin. "Light that fucker up and let them know not to mess with the Badlands PPD!"

We swerved hard right, and I nearly tumbled off the Deadhaul. Doe grabbed me at the last second and pulled me down.

"Going somewhere, Chief?"

"Thanks," I said. "Get ready to take out those Sweepers. I'll call the craters. Go!"

Doe moved to the end of the Deadhaul as Butch continued laying down cover fire.

"Lock her up, Butch!" I said over my connector. *"That Sweeper is close, and Doe is going to bring the pain!"*

"Ready!" Doe yelled. "Just say when, Chief."

I timed the swerves as Rose maneuvered the craters appearing in front of us. At first, it appeared completely random. After a few seconds, I was able to spot the pattern.

"On my mark, Doe!" I said, waiting for the swerve pattern to steady. We had a small window of four seconds before another crater would emerge. "Now!"

Doe fired a rocket at the lead Sweeper. He then immediately plunged another rocket in the launcher, firing a second time. Both rockets punched into the Hellion Sweeper, shredding it to pieces as it exploded all over the road.

The explosion took out a few more vehicles with it, but we still had two Sweepers to deal with.

I was about to load up my launcher, when I saw something race out of the rear of the Deadhaul.

"Butch, I told you to lock it up!"

"I tried, Chief but he was too fast," Butch replied. *"I'm sorry, Chief, I couldn't stop him."*

He? I looked up slowly at the Sweepers.

There, attached to the grill of the lead Hellion Sweeper, clung Pear.

CHAPTER 44

"**F**uckfuckfuck," I said, handing my rocket launcher to Doe. Part of my brain realized that I was beginning to sound like my little brother. *"I need to get him back. Hold all of your fire. I repeat hold all fire!"*

There was a loud crash and an explosion from the rear of the caravan as vehicles exploded in every direction.

"*Badlands up ahead, ten miles,*" Rose yelled. "*Dark Succubus, get your ass over here and help us shake these Sweepers!*"

"*Negative, Bloody Rose,*" Graffon answered. "*One of my axles suffered damage on our landing after the Mobius strip. We have to secure these weapons. I'm staying out of firing range.*"

"*Damn it!*" Rose yelled. "*Affirmative, Dark Succubus, keep your truck away from gunfire. We need those weapons. Chief, we're on our own.*"

"*Not entirely,*" I said, keeping an eye on Pear as more

cars and vehicles exploded at the end of the caravan. *"Seems like someone is wrecking it from behind."*

"That's what she said!" Silk yelled. We all laughed that time.

"Unholy hell," yelled out Butch, *"is that Bernard?"*

I used my sight and focused.

It *was* Bernard.

He was in a Hellion Sweeper.

"Can't leave you fuckers alone for ten minutes before you cockup the whole operation!" Bernard's voice came over the Deadhaul's radio, which I could just barely hear due to my enhanced hearing. "I'm coming in hot, Thorny, so get your ass out of the way."

"Bernie," Rose said, "how the hell did you get a Sweeper?"

"Story for another day, right now tell the chief to get his little brother off that Sweeper before he's paste."

"I'm on it," I said through the connector.

"You can hear the radio from up there?" Rose asked, and then quickly added, *"Scratch that. Fucking dragons."*

I grinned and jumped off the Deadhaul, forming my wings while aiming for Pear. I slammed into the Sweeper as my little brother transformed and made his way inside. The drivers of the Sweeper lasted five gruesome seconds before Bernard sideswiped it.

I grabbed Pear, nearly losing my grip due to the blood, and pulled him out of the cab. Then, I jumped again.

Pear looked like he wanted to shred me.

But he suddenly looked confused.

"Zeezee?" he asked, blinking at me. "Why are we out here?"

We landed on the roof of our Deadhaul with a roll as Bernard rammed his Sweeper into more vehicles. The road opened up and I could see Infernal City in the distance. Butch unleashed more mini-gun fury as Doe released another barrage of rockets. We were a moving cloud of explosions and bullets as we raced into the city.

It wasn't long before we convinced our pursuers that taking on the Badlands PPD would be the last mistake of their short lives. The few who remained pulled off and swerved away from us as we entered the city.

We raced down the Strip and to the station.

I used my sight and looked ahead.

"Stop the cars...now!" I commanded over the group channel.

They skidded to a halt with me and Doe holding on for dear life.

I climbed down the side, putting Pear in through the window before me.

Then, as I took my seat, I stared breathlessly into the distance.

"What in all that's unholy, Chief!" Rose said with a glare. We were still on the outskirts of the city. "You want to stop now? Now that we're almost home?"

"Do you see what I see?" I asked Rose as she stared at me in disbelief.

"I see a chief who has lost his mind," Rose snapped. "That's what I see."

"What's the hold up?" Bernard asked over the radio. "Did you forget something back at the wall?"

"Chief has eyes on something...sit tight." Rose responded.

Doe hit the ground and padded around Graffon's Deadhaul, hopping back inside.

"You see it?" I asked.

"I don't have dragon eyes, so probably not." She paused for a few seconds. "You going to let me in on the secret, or should I just throw a few turds against the wall to see what sticks?"

"Let's just say that it ain't good."

"Well, that clears it up. Thanks."

"Everyone out," I said over the connectors. *"Now."*

"What's up, Chief?" Silk asked.

"We have a situation."

CHAPTER 45

The Badlands Paranormal Police Department building looked like it had been transformed into an armory. Brand new fencing lined the perimeter, there were guards walking outside *and* inside, and there were even a few towers. And, unless my eyes were tricking me, there were even turrets and slow moving cameras at each major fence post.

Honestly, I felt kind of intimidated by the amount of work that Lieutenant Bradley had put in.

Now, it could have just been that he was some sort of project management dynamo, but I would never even have considered putting up this much of a blockade around headquarters.

Rose had grabbed her binoculars and was scanning the area as well.

"Holy fuck," she breathed. "Did you order Bradley to do all that?"

"Not even a portion of it," I replied.

"Holyfuckholyfuckholyfuck!" giggled Pear.

"Silence," Rose stated.

He obeyed.

"I'm assuming you're all seeing the amount of security surrounding the PPD building?" Graffon asked through the connector.

"We do," I answered, *"and, no, I didn't task Bradley with setting any of this up. This was all his doing."*

"Interesting," said Graffon. *"I'm curious as to where he got the funding for it all."*

That was a good point.

I knew that our budget wasn't even close to being able to afford the advanced tech I was seeing, and the very fact that all of this had been installed so fast would have easily quadrupled the costs.

A buzzing sounded through my connector. It was something I'd never heard before.

"Uh…" I said, looking over at Rose. "I think someone is trying to make my head explode."

She looked at me. "What do you mean?"

"My connector is buzzing," I replied. "At least it feels like that."

"That's a secure call," she stated. "Answer it."

"Right," I agreed with a nod. Then, added, "How do I do that again?"

"RTFM, Chief," she growled, meaning that I should Read The Fucking Manual. "Just focus on it. It'll ask you for your PIN."

"Got it," I said, focusing in on the buzzing. It asked for my PIN. "Okay, so…any idea what my PIN is?"

She facepalmed. "It's your Personal Identification Number, for fu…fudge's sake."

"I *know* that, Rose. I just don't know what the actual number is."

"You haven't set one up, yet?"

"Apparently not," I shot back.

"Then it's your badge number," she said, her head shaking at me with deep disapproval. "They'll just let anyone be the chief these days, won't they?"

I ignored her and mentally entered my badge number.

The buzzing stopped.

"*Chief Phoenix, this is the station calling,*" said the voice of Rowena. It was normalized again, which told me that she was no longer suffering the YODA complex. "*The building has been compromised. Do not cross the line of demarcation, or your vehicles will be targeted and shredded.*"

I knew Bradley's efficiency was too good to be true. He wasn't *helping* the PPD, he was taking the damn thing over.

Rose was right.

Bernard was right.

I was most decidedly wrong.

Swell.

But there was no way that Bradley was doing this on his own. It just wasn't possible. Again, the PPD budget alone would have afforded him maybe an eighth of what I was seeing here.

"*I'm assuming that nobody can hear us since you're using a secured channel, right?*" I asked, just to be sure.

"*That's kind of the point of a secured channel, Chief,*" Rowena replied.

"*Right. Any suggestions as to what we should do here?*"

"*I am connecting Nimble.*"

"Oh, okay."

A few seconds later, my lead technician joined the conference.

"Chief Phoenix?"

"Yes, Nimble, it's me. Are you in the building? Are the other officers in there with you? What about Tam and Yarrl? How many—"

"Chief," he interrupted, *"I can't answer all your questions at once. Let me just start by saying that all of the actual officers are in cells. I am also in a cell. Tam and Yarrl are in separate isolation cells."*

"Shit."

"Indeed," he replied. *"Bradley lost a number of his 'officers' while trying to subdue Tam and Yarrl."*

I had no doubt of that. They were quite a handful, after all.

"We need to get in there and free everyone," I said, even though it was obvious. *"Is there some hidden entrance like the one we used to escape the building?"*

"That's the only one I'm aware of, Chief," Nimble replied, *"and I can assure you it's under heavy guard now. The only way you're getting in here is through the use of heavy artillery."*

"We have some goodies," I pointed out. *"Two truck loads, in fact."*

"And if you use them, you'll get in," Nimble said, *"but you'll kill most of us in the process, so I'd appreciate it if you didn't actually use heavy artillery."*

Valid.

The problem was that we had to find a way in. I couldn't just let my officers sit in cells waiting for... whatever it was that Bradley had planned.

And, again, there was no way that Bradley was behind all this.

"Masters," I said aloud, snapping my fingers.

"Duh," replied Rose, her eyes still glued to the binoculars. "I told you he was vengeful as fu...fudge. Blowing up our weapons cache was cute, but this is where he's really going to turn the screws."

"You were right," I admitted.

"Yup."

"I just had no idea how deep Masters would take it."

"Phrasing."

"*All right, Nimble,*" I said, ignoring her, "*we're going to need to find a place to hide out while we plan.*"

"*There aren't many options for such—*"

"*I already have an idea,*" I interrupted. "*Just hang tight and be careful. If you can keep every one of the* actual *cops in line, do it, but don't let anyone know that we're out here planning. We still don't know who is really on our side and who isn't.*"

I could only assume that Nimble genuinely was on our side.

"*Will do, Chief,*" he replied. "*Good luck.*"

"*You, too,*" I said.

After explaining everything that Nimble had said to Rose, she pursed her lips and nodded slowly.

"Any suggestions on where we can hide?" I asked.

"Nope."

"Maybe House Blaze would—"

"Don't even think about it, Chief," Rose stopped me. "That'd be like me suggesting we go spend time with the valkyries."

I choked at the thought.

"Got it." Then I had a lightbulb moment. "What about Percy?"

"What about him?"

"He might know of a place," I said. "He's been a pretty good friend since I've gotten here. One of only a few, in fact."

Rose shrugged. "Worth a shot. Of course, he could have been playing you all this time, which means he'll welcome us in with open arms, and then we'll be slaughtered."

"You're one of those 'glass half-full' people, Rose. You know that?"

CHAPTER 46

I used my connector to call directly to Percy's business line. It was the only number I had for him.

"*Dirty Goblin,*" he answered. "*Percy here. Whatcha need?*"

"*Percy, it's me, Zeke. Please don't—*"

"*Zeke, old boy,*" he bellowed, "*what can I do you for?*"

"*—say my name.*"

"*I just said your name,*" he replied, sounding confused. "*You want me to say it again.... Hey, wait, this isn't some kind of weird sex call where you ask me to say your name while you're...you know?*"

"*What? No!*"

"*Good. I've already had three calls like that this week. I swear, I'm going to have to start charging for those.*"

"*First off,*" I said sourly, "*ew. Secondly, I'm asking you not to say my name aloud.*"

"*Well, that's a new twist on the game,*" he mused.

"*Percy, I'm not asking you to be involved in some weird sex*" act," I explained in a tight voice. *"I'm asking to not say my name because I'm trying to stay underground here."*

"Ah," he replied. *"That makes more sense. I didn't take you as the kinky type, Ze...uhhh...Zelda. But you never know with dragons."*

Great, now we were going to be adding 'Zelda' to the number of nicknames people had for me.

"So, what gives?" Percy asked.

"Lieutenant Bradley," I answered, *"probably under the direction of Masters, has taken over the PPD's headquarters. He's imprisoned the real officers and has his criminal cartel wearing badges and uniforms."*

"Explains why Bradley was in here last night looking for recruits. I thought it was odd, but with this being the Badlands and all, I just kind of let it go."

Nothing good comes from the Badlands.

Those words were imprinting more and more on my brain lately.

Ugh.

"Look," I said, trying to keep the desperation out of my voice, *"we need a place to plan. Somewhere safe, or at least defensible."*

"Say no more," Percy replied. *"Seriously. Say no more. Let me talk. You listen, and listen carefully."* He cleared his throat, after I heard a door close. *"I'm out of the main area now, Zelda. Nobody can hear me in here."*

"Then why are you still calling me Zelda?"

"Right. Sorry. Anyway, I'm guessing you ended up with the weapons you needed?"

"Yeah, we have two Deadhauls full of them."

"Good," he replied. *"Hide those Deadhauls and remove the*

tracking devices. Bury those devices somewhere out in the desert. Then get your asses over to Fang Park. Go to the Gay Vampire Fountain and twist the balls on the statue."

"What?"

"Just do it," he insisted. "It'll open up a panel at the edge of the fountain. Climb down and follow it all the way to the end. You'll see a green button. Press it, and I'll open the door for you."

"Where are you sending us, exactly?"

"Under the Dirty Goblin," he replied. "You'll be safe here. Now, I gotta get back out there before anyone gets suspicious. Trolls don't take an hour to drop a deuce like you human-types."

"Ew."

"Tell me about it," he laughed. "I'll keep an eye out for the signal. Good luck."

"Thanks," I groaned. "We'll need it."

"Yep."

CHAPTER 47

*B*ernard had removed the tracking devices from the Deadhauls and the Hellion Sweeper. He opened the back of the Sweeper and drove a smaller vehicle out the back of it, revealing even more weaponry inside the monstrous beast.

Then, he drove the tracking devices far out into the desert, returning after about twenty minutes. He assured us that they were so far buried that it'd take The Morgue weeks to find them.

While he was gone, we had effectively camouflaged the vehicles, after taking as much weaponry as we could safely carry.

"Now what?" asked Rose.

"We go to Fang Park and twist the balls on the Gay Vampire Fountain," I answered, reading off my notes.

She just blinked.

"What?" I said. "That's what Percy said we had to do in order to open the secret passageway."

Bernard laughed. "It'd work on me."

We all piled into Bernard's vehicle. He sped across town, pulling into a dark area near the park.

It wasn't much of a recreational area. There were mainly bushes and a few benches, aside from the fountain in the middle.

"Which set are we supposed to twist?" Rose asked as we stared at the seven different vampire statues, all of which looked identical.

"I have no idea," I replied with a sigh. "I guess we twist each set until we find the one that opens the floodgates."

"Phrasing," she muttered, and then declared, "I think I'll sit this one out, Chief. You go ahead and do what you have to do."

Everyone else stood there with their arms crossed as well.

Nice.

"Fine," I said, frowning at them. "Just remember that I'm doing this to save our asses."

"Very noble," Rose said. "Now, less talky talky and more gropey gropey."

I rolled my eyes and began walking from statue to statue, grabbing each set of rock testicles and attempting to twist them. My crew took the opportunity to laugh with every attempt.

As Mr. Murphy and his Law would have it, none of them budged until I reached the last statue.

"This one must be the mother load," I called out as I felt the rock begin to turn.

Many of the crew giggled. Honestly, they were like children.

As soon as I began twisting the testes-of-rock, the

appendage part of the statue's member twisted as well, moving to point upwards.

Alpha One and Alpha Two were literally on the ground in laughter.

Whoever designed this thing was an asshole.

The sound of scraping could be heard as I continued twisting the statue's sack.

I looked over and saw that an entrance had opened near the edge of the fountain. That's where our escape hatch was.

"I see the opening," I called out, silencing their laughter. "It'll be a tight fit, but I'm sure we can squeeze in there if we take our time."

The laughter resumed.

CHAPTER 48

The tunnel had run a solid mile. I didn't know if Percy had built it himself, had it built, or inherited it from someone else when he'd taken over the Dirty Goblin, but I was sure glad it was there.

I reached out and pressed the green button, hoping for the best.

A few seconds later, a part of the wall slid open, revealing a relatively nice place hidden inside. It was clean, had multiple places to sit, sported a large screen TV, and there were tables, drinks, and food.

All in all, it was a decent hideout.

"Not too shabby," said Rose. "I don't want to know exactly what this place is intended for, being that we got here by you playing with the junk on a gay vampire statue in Fang Park, but it's cozy."

"Yeah," I agreed…with both of her points. I checked my datapad and connector signal. "We have full access from here, too. That means we'll be able to plan our next steps."

"Which will be what, exactly?" Bernard asked as Pear sidled up next to him and took his hand.

So weird.

"I don't know yet, Bernard," I replied. "One thing is for sure, though...I'm going to need every person on this team to chip in."

"Why's that?" asked Rose.

"Because I'm learning more and more that I don't know enough about the Badlands," I admitted. "I'm a little *too* honorable."

Everyone in the room nodded in agreement.

With that, I sighed and sat down.

I only had a skeleton crew to work with, but these people were solid. That included Bernard, though I wasn't sure how far he was going to go in with us. Oddly enough, I was hoping he'd stick around until we got the PPD back on its feet. He was solid, but more importantly, he could control Pear.

"We have a lot of planning to do," Rose said, sitting next to me as the rest of the crew started digging through the refrigerator.

I nodded slowly. "Think we can get it back?"

"The precinct?"

"Yeah."

"Not a clue," she replied, "but it'll be fun to try."

I gave her a sidelong glance. "You have a strange idea of fun, Rose."

"Probably," she acceded. "You have to admit that running the gauntlet like we just did was a blast."

"Not even a little bit," I replied, dead serious, "but I'm not a hellion."

"No, you're definitely not," she agreed, a grin forming on her face. "You did okay, though...for a dragon."

I raised an eyebrow. "High praise, coming from you."

We turned back to look at the team. They were fighting over a bag of chips. It was getting pretty serious.

Pear walked into the middle of the fray and growled.

That silenced everyone.

Slowly, Silk handed my little brother the chips and then stepped back. He took them over to Bernard, who was all smiles.

Tricky.

"Better keep an eye on him," Rose laughed.

"Which one?"

"Both."

I smiled at that.

Somehow—and I had no idea precisely *how* just yet—we were going to have to come up with a plan that landed the PPD precinct back in our hands. It wasn't going to be easy, and it sure as hell wasn't going to be pretty, but it had to happen.

The Badlands needed us to do it, whether they knew it or not.

...whether they *wanted* it or not.

But that wasn't a task for today.

I'd just been through the most stressful road trip imaginable. My life had passed before my eyes more times than I could count. It was harrowing, nail-biting, and bloody.

Planning the venture of taking back the PPD was going to need to wait a little while.

"We should figure it all out first, Chief," Rose said.

"Everyone's tired. We need to reenergize, plan things out right, and then go in guns blazing."

"Agreed," I affirmed. "No sense in rushing into a fight that we're not prepared for."

"Nope."

I pushed myself up from the chair and addressed the room.

"Good work today, gang," I said. "I know we're not done, but we got the weapons we needed. Not all of them, no, but enough to tide us over to the next shipment."

"We do still need to get the precinct back, sir," Graffon stated.

"That we do, Graffon," I agreed. "With any luck, we'll be able to seize additional weapons from Bradley and his crew when we do. For now, though, we all need some rest. We need to plan logically and thoroughly if we're to have a chance of gaining control back."

"I could use a few...hundred beers," Silk added, falling back onto one of the couches.

"Pizza," suggested Doe.

"Ah, hell yeah," agreed Silk, pointing at the void.

"Maybe Percy can arrange something," I said, calming the chatter. "In the meantime, we need to recover. In three days time, we're going to get our damn precinct back. I need everyone at the top of their game when we do that."

I looked from face to face, thinking that if there was any one crew in the Badlands who were capable of facing what we were up against, it was Alpha Team.

"What about you, Chief?" asked Doe.

I looked at him. "What do you mean?"

"You've pointed out that you're learning a lot from us,

and you've recognized that being in the Badlands means that your Boy Scout act isn't always the best play."

Count on Doe for getting straight to the heart of things.

"Yeah?" I pressed.

"He's asking what you're planning to do to change it," Rose groaned.

"As to that," I answered, my voice going cold, "Masters has just put me in a difficult position. He doesn't know it, but he's just forced me to push away some of my honor."

My eyes smoldered.

"That's right, people," I announced powerfully as I sought to build up my team for what was to come over the next few days, "it's time to open up and let something big and nasty enter me."

I cringed the moment I'd said it.

"Phrasing!"

~

The End

~

Thanks for Reading

If you enjoyed this book, would you please leave a review at the site you purchased it from? It doesn't have to be a book report… just a line or two would be fantastic and it would really help us out!

John P. Logsdon
www.JohnPLogsdon.com

John was raised in the MD/VA/DC area. Growing up, John had a steady interest in writing stories, playing music, and tinkering with computers. He spent over 20 years working in the video games industry where he acted as designer and producer on many online games. He's written science fiction, fantasy, humor, and even books on game development. While he enjoys writing lighthearted adventures and wacky comedies most, he can't seem to turn down writing darker fiction.

Orlando A. Sanchez
www.orlandoasanchez.com

Orlando has been writing ever since his teens when he was immersed in creating scenarios for playing Dungeon and Dragons with his friends every weekend. The worlds of his books are urban settings with a twist of the paranormal lurking just behind the scenes and generous doses of magic, martial arts, and mayhem. He currently resides in Queens, NY with his wife and children and can often be found lurking in the local coffee shops where most of his writing is done.

CRIMSON MYTH PRESS

Crimson Myth Press offers more books by this author as well as books from a few other hand-picked authors. From science fiction & fantasy to adventure & mystery, we bring the best stories for adults and kids alike.

www.CrimsonMyth.com

Made in the
USA
Middletown, DE